D1752620

GEORGIA

GEORGIA

PHOTOGRAPHY • JAMES VALENTINE

TEXT • CHARLES WHARTON

International Standard Book Number 0-912856-35-1
Library of Congress Catalog Number 77-96964
Copyright© 1977 by Publisher • Charles H. Belding
Graphic Arts Center Publishing Co.
2000 N.W. Wilson • Portland, Oregon • 503/224-7777
Designer • Robert Reynolds
Printer • Graphic Arts Center
Bindery • Lincoln & Allen
Printed in the United States of America

An ancient oak bows before a rising fire.
South End Beach, Ossabaw Island.

Together the needles of the pond cypress and cinnamon fern spread their essences into a small enchanted corner of the south.
Middle Fork, Okefenokee National Wildlife Refuge.

A crisp field of dried flowers replenishes the spirit. Resaca Sugar Valley Road. Pages 8 and 9: This unusual grass gets its vibrant reddish-pink color from excess food production not used during the fall. Found on St. Catherine's Island.

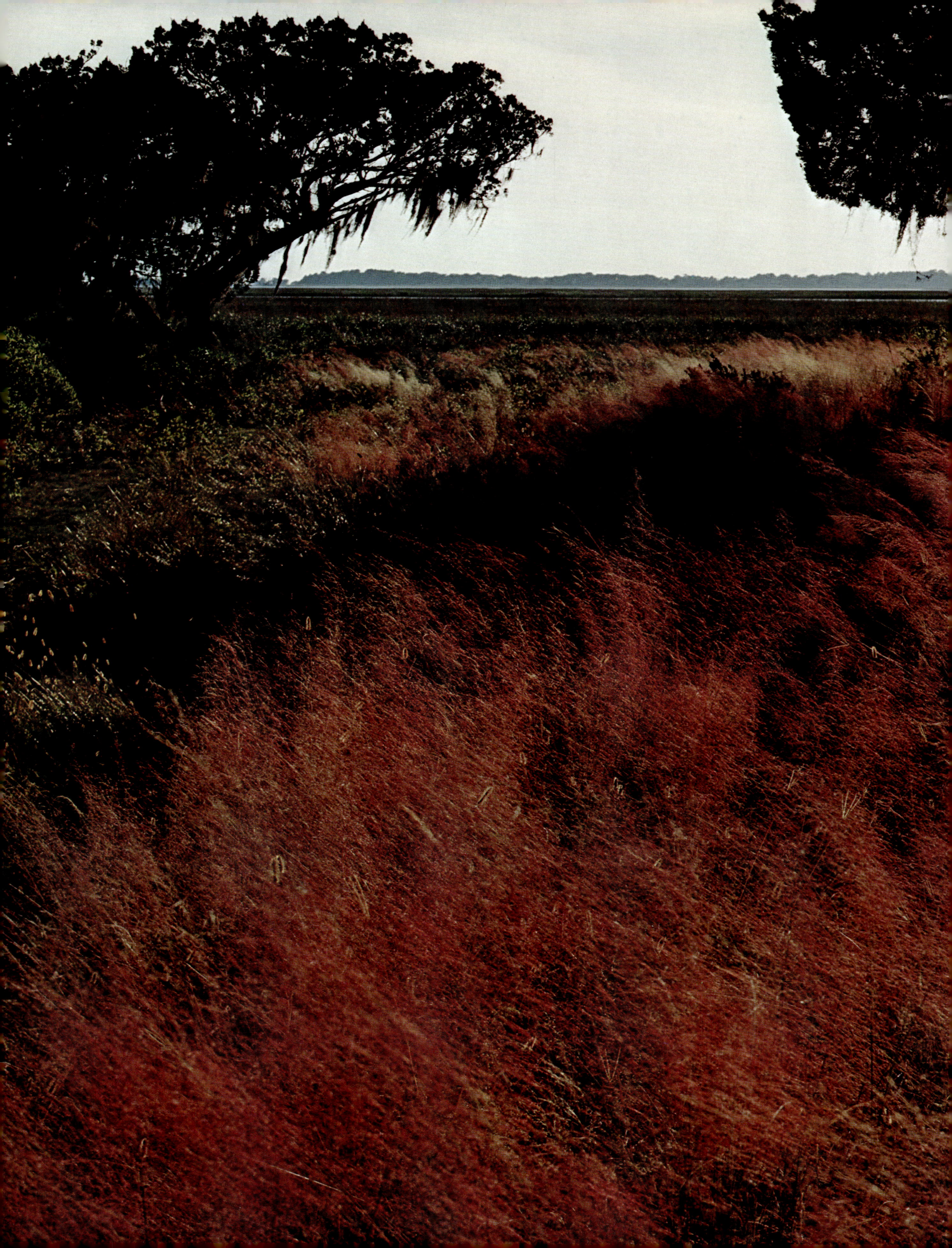

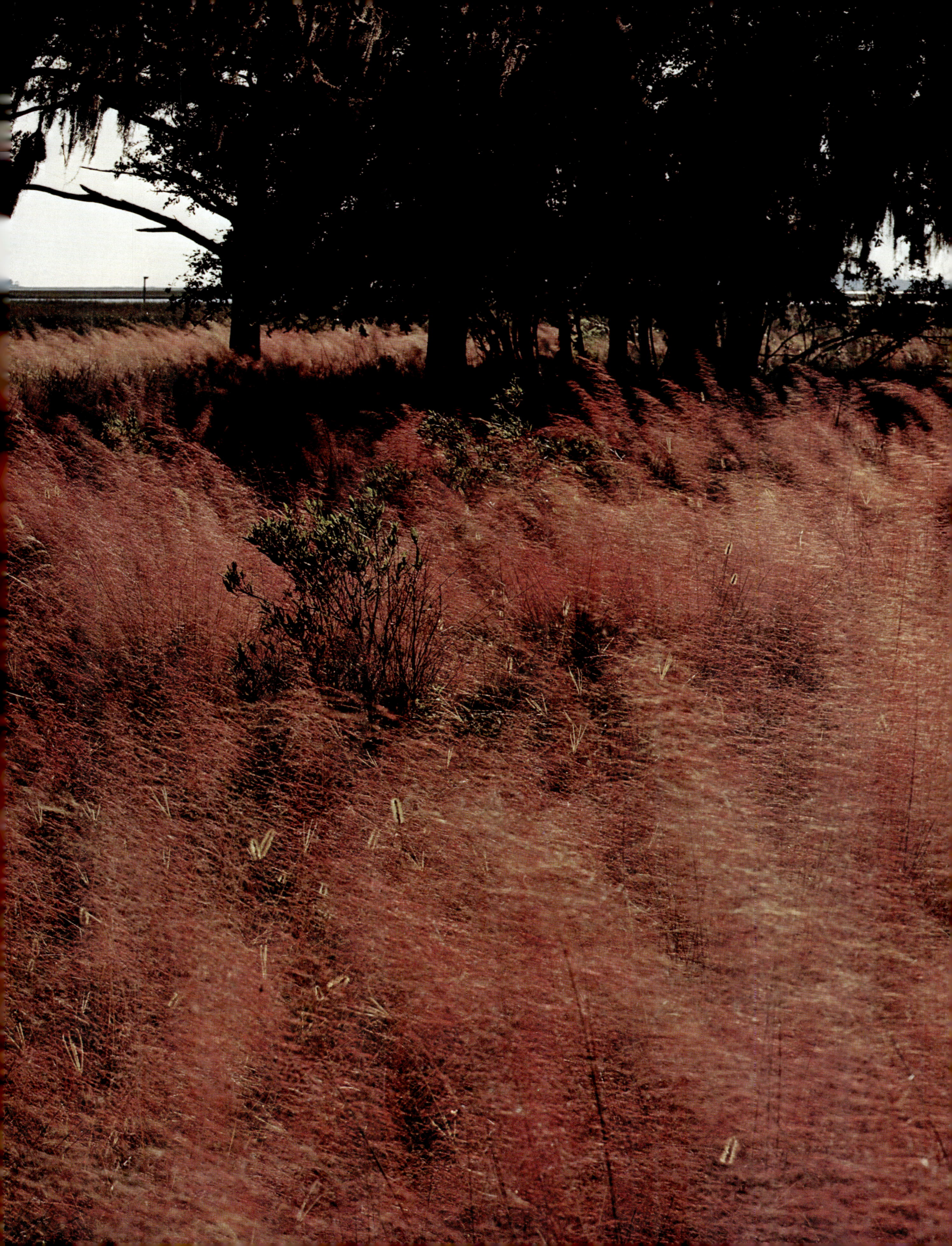

A rustic barn melts back into the Appalachian landscape near the Richard Russell Scenic Highway.

Early morning veil of fog, Rabun Gap, Dillard.
Pages 12 and 13: Heggie Rock, ancient granite outcrop emerging from the soft Piedmont. The roughly 60 acre outcrop near Augusta is composite of dish gardens; pines and cedars gnarled and twisted by exposure; lichens and mosses pulling nutrients from the ageless rock.

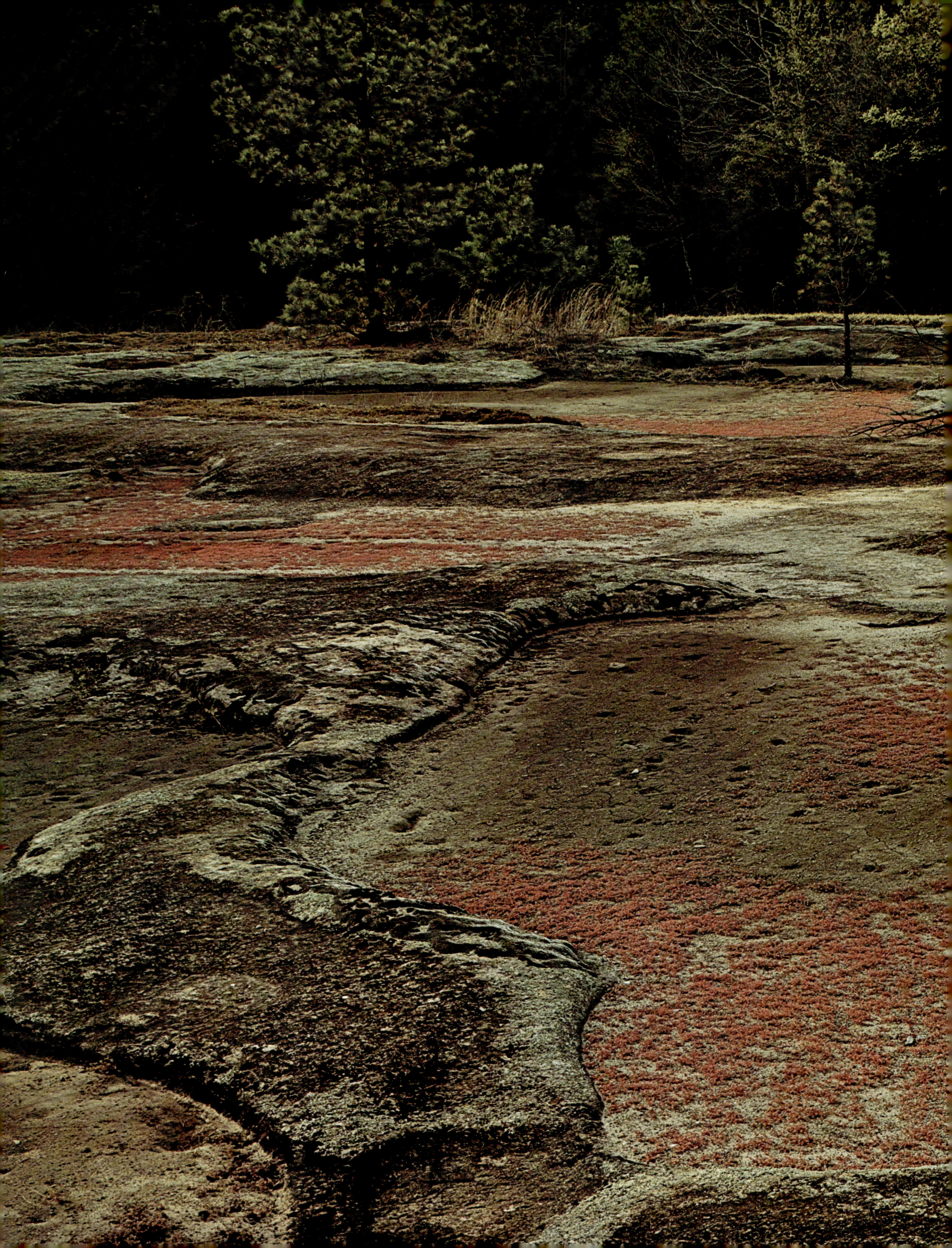

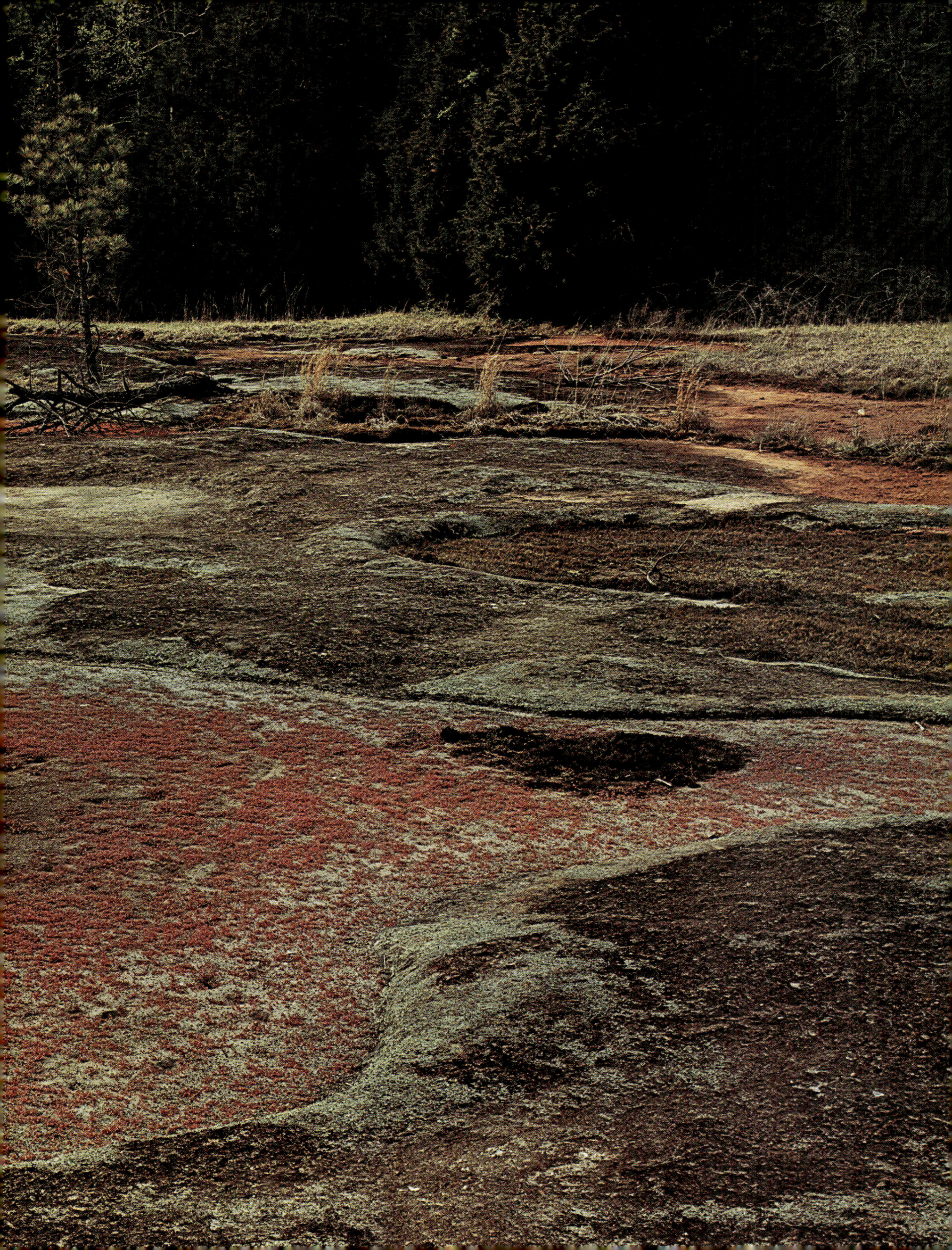

A titi shrub forest casts its snow-white blossoms over a sky-filled rain pond spattered with yellow bladderwort near, Manor.

A potpourri of rhododendron, and mountain
laurel, highlight the green leafy cliffs of
Cloudland Canyon State Park, near Rising Fawn.

This carefully ornamented canyon forms a unique cove for Dukes Creek to play in. Dukes Creek Falls on the Richard Russell Scenic Highway.

THE BLUE RIDGE PROVINCE

The Blue Ridge bursts into Georgia along the edge of the Highlands Plateau. Our 4,696-foot Rabun Bald, the state's second highest peak, stands guard at the point of entry. Just east of the Rabun Bald the Chattooga River terminates the greatest series of gorges in eastern America. Of these spectacular gorges the Toxaway, Horsepasture, Whitewater and Chattooga Rivers form the most outstanding. These gorges are formed where mountain streams plunge off the sharp escarpment edge of the Blue Ridge. Subject of much study by biologists based at the Highlands Biological Laboratory, these gorges contain some extremely rare ferns and one plant, the Oconee bells, found nowhere else in the world. The Chattooga has wild and scenic river status. The origin of the east fork is presided over by the monolith of Whiteside Mountain, and enters the state in the Ellicott's Rock Wilderness where the three states join in the extreme northeast corner. After the surveyor Ellicott had ventured in on horseback to establish the corner, the Georgia-North Carolina line was surveyed. In Ellicott's Rock Wilderness the botanist DuMond describes a virgin stand of hemlock and tulip poplar with stem diameters of four to four and one-half feet. From this relatively inaccessible point the Chattooga is a magnificent trout stream descending through pools, falls and along striking cliffs until it joins the Tallulah to form the Savannah River. Lower sections three and four rate among the finest whitewater adventures in America. Three major outfitters regularly lead intrepid crash-helmeted visitors on heart-stopping raft trips through the roaring and tossing rapids, also a major kayak run. Fishermen seeking giant brown trout are sometimes greeted by the mangled remnants of aluminum canoes along sections where only the experienced should venture. James Dickey's novel *Deliverance* was filmed largely on the Chattooga. On the porch of Clayton's Dilliard Motor Lodge is a sign which daily records the water level for the benefit of the swarm of adventurers who assemble there, their cars laden with canoes, kayaks, and rafts of every make and color. The Chattooga's west fork rises in the isolated Blue Valley. A small protected zone, the Three Forks Wilderness, guards the heart of some rugged country, exposing boulders as large as mountain cabins. The cliff and slopes support characteristic environments.

Along the Chattooga hemlock and white pine are the dominant trees except in coves where the soil is deep enough for oak, poplar and buckeye. Rosebay rhododendron and mountain laurel dominate the shrub layer. One spectacular tree is the *Stewartia*, or mountain camelia, which occurs along the Chattooga and tributaries.

From Rabun Bald the mountains sweep around the headwaters of the Tallulah River. At this point the Blue Ridge intersects the imposing Nantahala Range which stretches northward towards the Great Smokies. The term *nantahala* is derived from the Cherokee "Nunda-ayeli" meaning Land of the Noonday Sun, referring to the deep gorges where the sun shines only at midday. Here in a great sinuous double arc the Appalachian Trail courts closely the Georgia line along Ridgepole, Standing Indian, Big Laurel and then straightens out in a southwest course at the juncture of the Hightower Bald lead coming in from the west. Together, the peaks and high country on the headwaters of the Tallulah and Nantahala Rivers comprise a prime candidate for wilderness and back country status. Here the mountain lion ranges into Georgia, being found as far south as the U.S. Highway 76 crossing at Dick's Creek Gap on the Towns-Rabun County line. In this mountain mass, more properly called the southern Nantahalas, and lying north of U.S. Highway 76, many northern or boreal animals reach the southern limits of their range. These include not only two endangered species, the eastern cougar and the bog turtle, but number among them the wood frog, pygmy shrew, red-backed vole and red squirrel or "boomer" as they are known to the mountaineers.

The Tallulah River itself is a fascinating tributary of the Savannah. Its headwaters drain the wild country of the cougar, black bear and European wild boar. Descending into Rabun County it traverses the Rock Mountain Gorge. A highly scenic drive blasted from solid rock to reach the rich timber of the watershed wends its way along seven miles of roaring cascades, falls and pools. Stocked weekly, it is Georgia's most popular trout stream. After passing through a chain of four narrow power lakes the stream drops down into the 1200 foot chasm of Tallulah Gorge. Here around the gorge two rare trees, the Carolina hemlock and table mountain pine occur, with cracks in the cliffs inhabited by the unique green salamander. Tallulah is said to mean "terrible water" in the language of the Cherokee.

From where the Appalachian Trail crosses U.S. Highway 76 the Blue Ridge travels southwestward with numerous peaks above 4000 feet. It includes the wilderness arm of 4,568-foot Hightower, then crosses historic 4,458-foot Blood Mountain to the present end of the Appalachian Trail on 3,782-foot Springer Mountain, and terminates on the 3,290-foot Burnt-Oglethorpe Mountain massif. Georgia's 4,748-foot Brasstown Bald forms a notable northern offshoot of the Blue Ridge. From its top, dominated by shrub-bald vegetation and miniaturized trees, magnificent views are beheld for 360 degrees. The highway from Jack's Gap to the Forest Service parking lot near the visitor's center on top is one of Georgia's steepest grades. Here is an excellent place to see some of our mountain environments, and illustrates the remarkable contrast between north and south slopes. The south slopes of Brasstown Bald are dominated by an oak-hickory forest with species of the white and red oak groups most obvious. Near the top, on the south side, is a forest of white oaks dwarfed by high altitude, while rocky ridges and slopes at lower elevations are dominated by chestnut oak. The north face is another world. Here in a cold, northern clime, ancient yellow birches lichen-draped with old man's beard reign over a rhododendron understory where ice-fractured rocks and thin soil form a boulderfield, creating an unique "cloud forest."

Boulderfields occur at high elevations at the head of mountain coves where the soil is thin and cold and water gurgles deep underneath. These environments probably date back to the glacial ages of the Pleistocene. In places and lower down on the north face where black, rich soil accumulates, gardens of rare northern herbs, including lilies and orchids, excite the botanist. Trees like buckeye begin to be seen. Some special large ones can be viewed from State Highway 180 which, circling north of Blood and Slaughter Mountains, passes through the Sosebee Cove Scenic Area, established by the U.S. Forest Service. Here also can be eyed a grove of young tulip poplar, a tree which has come to dominate the forest since the logging of the oaks. Many mountain coves also became dominated by poplars with the death of the chestnut, caused by an Asiatic fungus which in the 30's swept down from New York State. Nearly a quarter of the forest trees of Appalachia succumbed, giving birth to "wormy chestnut", a derivative from these fallen monarchs that still commands a high price at the sawmill. Chestnuts also grew in the Georgia Piedmont. They provided abundant and delicious nuts that fattened turkey, deer and bear as well as the hogs that mountaineers kept loose in the forest. Chestnut and acorn-fattened pork was a special treat. At high elevations ghost forests of smaller dead chestnuts still stand, their stark, white "skeletons" often bear at their feet a new growth of sprouts and occasionally on the high ridges a ten-inch tree will bear a few nuts before it too succumbs to the omnipresent fungus. While the loss of the chestnut did remove a great wild food source it did not destroy the integrity of the ecosystem. It illustrates that the wisdom of having many species of trees is one of nature's strategies which evolution builds into climax forests to avoid catastrophic loss. Several years ago an elm spanworm outbreak destroyed vast numbers of hickories and certain oak species. Today the damage is scarcely noticeable although populations of mast-dependent animals, such as squirrels, may have been temporarily reduced.

Northwest of the Blue Ridge terminus in Gilmer County there lies a compact group of 4000 foot peaks called the Rich Mountain area. Northwest of the Rich Mountains lies the mass of the Cohuttas also identified by 4000 foot peaks and between them the Great Murphy Fault followed by U.S. Highway 76 from Blue Ridge to Ellijay. Within the Cohutta Mountains lie the headwaters of the Jacks and Conasauga Rivers, plus the 34,500 acre Cohutta Wilderness. The Cohuttas may be thought of as the southern terminus of the mountain range running south from the Great Smokies. Both the Rich and Cohutta Mountains bear similar environments to the main Blue Ridge.

One of the fascinating topics in the state's biology is the unique distribution of aquatic fauna in river systems. Streams draining northward into the Mississippi via the Tennessee have many colorful and characteristic species not found in the streams draining into the Gulf, such as the Coosa, or into the Atlantic. The fabled muskellunge is one species of fish restricted to Tennessee headwaters. These streams also contain the giant salamander, sometimes called the hellbender, reaching a length of 29 inches and a weight of several pounds. This grotesque animal is adapted to cold, oxygenated mountain rivers and lives beneath flat rocks.

The southern-most bastion of the Cohuttas is Fort Mountain, occupied by a state park. Here is a stone wall constructed by the Cherokees, who built low walls encircling a number of mountain peaks, probably delineating sacred or ceremonial areas. From the summit of Fort Mountain one gazes westward across a vast valley to the distant Armuchee Ridges. This ancient rift in the mountains is called the Great Valley, measuring from 15 to 25 miles in width; a geologic region of undeformed sedimentary rocks. Its eastern edge is the Great Smoky Fault which divides these very old sediments from the metamorphosed, mineralized rocks of the Blue Ridge, Cohuttas and Piedmont. Recent investigation reveals that the Great Valley contains numerous plants and animals characteristic of the Coastal Plain, 100 miles to the south. Cottonmouth moccasins, for example, occur very near the city of Rome. The Great Valley of the Coosa River has rendered and served as an animal pathway from the Coastal Plain of Alabama.

Crossing the Great Valley one encounters the long, low Armuchee Ridges. Sandstones and chert comprising them were more resistant to erosion than the surrounding rocks. West of the Armuchee Ridges is the 12 mile wide Chickamauga Valley noted for remarkable cedar glades and large springs in Catoosa County. West of this is the 1,000 foot wall of Lookout Mountain and its eastern fork, Pigeon Mountain. Lookout Mountain, recognized as our part of the Cumberland Plateau has a very flat top some ten miles wide, capped by a resistant sandstone which is especially obvious on the eastern rim along which

Highway 239 runs. Here one finds the sandstone weathered into globules, kettles, balanced rocks, spires and even things which resemble man-made carvings, forming a "rock city" type of weathering. The forest consists of dwarfed shortleaf pines and various oaks, bonsaied by the dry winds and impoverished soil.

The west side, which can be only partly followed by Highway 157, is a rocky slope supporting a dry hardwood forest dominated by chestnut oaks. Streams which originate on the top of Lookout Mountain often form spectacular falls or ravines as they plunge over the edge of the escarpment. Easily the most breathtaking of these is Cloudland Canyon, formerly called Sitton's Gulch, and now a state park. This deep gorge is carved in sandstones of Pennsylvania Age. The spectacular Daniel's Creek Falls can be walked behind because of an easily eroded bed of shale sandwiched between the sandstones. The hemlocks of Daniel's and Bear Creeks have a botanically unique association with the purple or catawba rhododendron, normally a mountain top form, instead of occurring with the pink rhododendron found throughout the ravines of the Blue Ridge.

PIEDMONT

The Piedmont is a broad zone of rolling hills between the mountains and the Coastal Plain, identified largely by its physiography or land-form. Geologically it is scarcely different from the mountains. The junction with the Coastal Plain is geologically distinct but difficult to "see" on the ground. The Piedmont ends about midway down the state. The cities of Columbus, Macon and Augusta are located at the boundary or "Fall Line" where early-day navigation generally ceased because of shoals. Because hills are characteristic of the upper Coastal Plain, it is often hard to judge when one leaves the Piedmont. Even the presence or absence of red clay is no help since there are red clays visible in road cuts of the Red Hills section of the Coastal Plain. Neither is the Piedmont a distinct biotic zone—for few plants or animals are confined to it. Rather, in Georgia at least, it seems to be a meeting place of some of the distinctive flora and fauna from the mountains and the Coastal Plain.

At places, such as coming down U.S. Highway 441 from Cornelia atop one of the Gainesville Ridges, a good panorama of the Piedmont can be seen. It is on these same steep ridges where one can see some of the original oak-hickory forest that clothed much of the Piedmont when Caucasian man arrived. Other sites where we can glimpse near-original vegetation is along the Chattahoochee bluffs. The most outstanding of these are called the Chattahoochee Palisades; a new state park protects some, and a more extensive river park concept would protect key wild areas northward to the Lake Lanier dam.

Piedmont bluff forests sometimes have rock shelters with evidence of continuous occupation by Indians. Much of the area northwest of Atlanta was never farmed and presents a near-original forest aspect. Parts of the 60-acre Fernbank Forest, in the Atlanta-Decatur area, are near-original and have been more or less protected since 1820. Tulip poplars on a bluff there are approximately 225 years of age. Nearby grow white oaks which are probably the most characteristic trees of moist Piedmont hardwood forests.

On many cold, moist bluffs along Piedmont rivers and creeks there originally grew a profusion of mountain shrubs and herbs. Along the Chattahoochee today, mountain laurel and rhododendron extend southward to Atlanta. Such mountain herbs as doll's eyes, goat's beard and the maidenhair fern were once apparently widespread in these plant communities. Two species of huge-leaved deciduous magnolia trees, which have evolved in southern environments, seem to be characteristic of near-original Piedmont ravine forests.

Perhaps the most remarkable of all biotic areas in Georgia is the Pine Mountain massif, through which the Flint River has cut its water gaps. Here in cool ravines and on moist slopes live a remarkable mixture of mountain and Coastal Plain plants. One can see Coastal Plain tupelo, Spanish moss and titi almost side by side with mountain laurel and ginseng. Even more perplexing is the occurence here of the Coastal Plain coral snake along with the purple salamander, a mountain form. But again an east-west trending mountain range with rocks which weather into sands instead of clays provides the opportunity for an unusual mixture of plants and animals in the lower Piedmont. Pine Mountain's resistant Hollis quartzite has backed the Flint River up into the Piedmont's largest river swamp complex. Aided by beavers and their abundant ponds, the Flint basin in the Piedmont evidently provides environments which have allowed the survival of some Coastal Plain animal life which normally does not occur elsewhere. For years I had heard persistent rumors of the venomous cottonmouth in the Flint swamps near Atlanta. In 1969 we discovered that these snakes do occur there not only just south of Atlanta but in pockets throughout the Flint basin, along with green tree frogs, mud snakes, bowfin fish and other uniquely Coastal Plain forms. The Flint Basin is not the only anomalous pocket of disjunct life in the Piedmont. The Alcovy River in Newton and Walton Counties has a small but beautiful swamp with such Coastal Plain forms as tupelo gum trees, mole salamanders and bird-voiced tree frogs. Though agriculture has utilized almost all of the Piedmont uplands, floodplain swamps along Piedmont streams such as the Alcovy and Flint, though narrow, have managed to survive the increased erosion from man's early, careless farming efforts. They survive as linear greenbelts, highly productive of plants and animals, doing vital work in purifying water for surrounding communities and providing high educational and recreational values.

While many Piedmont streams have floodplain forests along them they often have another distinctive feature called a shoal, where they cross more resistant rock structures, forming white-water rapids. Sections of the Broad River and the Chattahoochee have exciting areas of whitewater to the delight of canoeist and rafter. The section of the Flint River through Pine Mountain presents many miles of shoal water harboring a distinctive species, the shoal or Flint River bass. This section of the river has been found by biologists to produce more fish per fisherman than any other stream in Georgia. In earlier times the Indians harvested great quantities of clams from Piedmont river shoals. Indian fish weirs are still seen along the Flint River. Other streams such as Mulberry and Potato Creeks in the Pine Mountain area and Dog River and Sweetwater Creek south of Atlanta have distinctive shoals and sometimes, stunning falls. Most Piedmont streams have high water four times yearly in winter and spring that covers their floodplains, creating waterfalls and shoals rendering an awesome spectacle. It is said that the gorges of the Flint when in flood rival the Colorado and would be suicidal to float in boats.

It is the pine tree and the red clay that is often noted by the visitor riding across Georgia's Piedmont. The clay is derived from a major component of Piedmont rocks called feldspar, stained red by iron oxidized due to the abundant rainfall. Stands of pine trees in the mountains and Piedmont occur naturally only where soils are thin or where rocks are close to the surface. This confines pine normally to rocky ridges or where granite rocks lie close to the surface, producing greyish soils. Elsewhere they are opportunists and seem to either follow man around or take advantage of natural catastrophy such as a tornado or fire. Their rapid growing seedlings may seed into an opening produced by the blow down of an old oak in dry situations. In wetter situations tulip poplars with similar winged seeds are better able to survive. Following complete destruction of a deciduous forest by man, fire or other agency there occurs in the Piedmont region a remarkable forest recovery by stages known as "plant succession". Indeed, scientists from around the world have journeyed to the Piedmont to observe the process, which has been extensively studied by our state scientists. Essentially, a bare field goes through some or all of the following stages: weed, grass, shrub, pine seedling, pine forest dominated by loblolly, pine forest with oak-hickory seedlings, oak-hickory forest. Interestingly, animal life follows a similar successional pattern. Harvest mice which eat weed seeds are present in the weed stage, cotton rats which eat grass are present in the grass stage and deer mice which eat acorns are present in the final stage. Among the birds, early stages are dominated by meadow larks and sparrows, and the later stages by forest species such as red-eyed vireos and cardinals. The blue grosbeak occurs only in areas undergoing succession. Further, the number of bird species increases until about the 60th year, then steadies to about 19 species in the oak-hickory climax forest which is attained some time after 150 years. Insects and other invertebrates and the soil itself follow similar patterns of change, which gradually restore the diverse and stable ecosystem that maximizes the energy and nutrition that are available from the given climate and landform.

Of all the Piedmont environments, the granite outcrops attract the most attention. The first effort of the newly-formed Georgia Conservancy was to purchase Panola Mountain, a large outcrop in Henry County. Although granite outcrops are found in the Piedmont of other states, they are seemingly more numerous and larger in Georgia. Outcrops occur where the softer rocks and their soils have been eroded off of the underlying granitic bedrock. This massive shield of granite and layered granite called gneiss underlies much of the central Piedmont. Some counties such as Walton have over 150 outcrops with Green County reaching an average size of over 100 acres. Most outcrops are flat but some have rounded domes such as Panola, Arabia or Stone Mountain. Thus the mountains in the Piedmont that tend to rise above the general high surface are composed of rocks that are harder or more resistant. Some are of granite namely Stone Mountain, in DeKalb County. Others are of quartzite: Pine Mountain in Harris, Meriwether, Upson, and Pike Counties and Pine Log Mountain in Bartow and Cherokee Counties. Granite not only forms monolithic domes, but underlies vast areas of the Piedmont. Outcrops have been exposed so long that plants growing on them have undergone rapid genetic change and have become different species. Some plants occur only on Piedmont outcrops, other plants are shared with sandstone outcrops in the southern part of the state. One 92-acre outcrop in Columbia County, Heggies Rock, has been described as the most outstanding potential natural landmark site in eastern America, and contains 11 of 19 plant species endemic to granite outcrops.

One plant, the vividly yellow confederate daisy, grows only on granite outcrops. The outcrops are not only natural laboratories, where local scientists are studying genetic change but they are yielding other secrets of life. Many granite outcrops bear numerous shallow pits or eroded basins filled with varying depths of soil. This soil, incidentally, is formed in situ practically before the eyes of fascinated students. The basic rocks contain about 22 minerals which weather by the action of freeze-thaw and carbonic acid in rainwater; contributing most of the basic elements needed by life. Others not found in the granite such as nitrogen, iodine and sulfur are added by fall-out or later, by the plants and animals themselves. Thus the outcrops present the steps of primordial soil formation, eventually permitting pine trees to grow high on the naked granite slopes of Stone Mountain. Primitive lichens and mosses growing on the rock surface also assist in the breakdown of the minerals. Accumulations of this new soil in shallow basins result in veritable dish gardens of primary plant succession, as opposed to secondary succession following catastrophic destruction. Plant succession in these "mini-ecosystems" begins with lichens through mosses to succulent annuals such as the spectacular pink to red stonecrop then, as the soil deepens, perennial herbs such as broomsedge and groundsels replace the annuals and finally the little dish gardens become dominated by shrubs and, eventually, pine trees. Outcrop animals are less well known. There is a grasshopper which is colored so as to be indistinguishable from the grey-green lichen-covered rock. Among the vertebrates small lizards predominate.

COASTAL PLAIN

The great Savannah River, whose headwaters we have seen partly gathered in the scenic gorges of Tallulah and Chattooga, seems reluctant to disassociate itself with the mountains. As it begins to cross the softer sediments of Coastal Plain hills it erodes high bluffs. Some face north, and support lush forests, the plants of which bear northern affinities. The most remarkable of these is Shell Bluff in Burke County. William Bartram himself discovered deposits of giant, fossilized oyster shells here, many specimens well over a foot in length. Even as far south as Three Sister's Ferry not far north of Savannah the bluffs bear mountain laurel and other plants who found cool niches where the seeds brought by the river from the distant Blue Ridge could flourish deep within the Coastal Plain. Few other state rivers have such exotic bluffs, although along the Chattahoochee in the extreme southwest corner of the state are the *torreya ravines*, containing Piedmont salamanders species and the stinking cedar, or *torreya*, a very rare member of the yew family and restricted to this remnant evolutionary pocket along the Apalachicola bluffs of Florida and Georgia. The Chattahoochee has some other exciting ravine forests farther north in Clay and Early Counties. Streams here, such as Kolomoki and Coheelee, cut gorges in laminated, soft clay or marl containing chert nodules up to washtub size. Roland Harper thought this part of Georgia distinctive enough to call it the "Blue Marl Region".

Georgia's great alluvial rivers such as the Savannah and the Altamaha have for millenia carried clays from the Piedmont, depositing them in vast swamps up to five miles wide. These swamps begin abruptly at the Fall Line, where the Flint, Ocmulgee and Oconee particularly, form their greatest swamps. Although there have been drainage schemes by the colonial agriculturalists and modern wood-using industry, the swamps form the nuclei for diverse wild riches and experiences, for so much of Georgia has become a vast farm of pine trees. These great swamps narrow as the rivers cross the vital recharge zone for the underground aquifer, then widen again. These green corridors of wilderness fringe most rivers in the Coastal Plain. "Swamps" are made up of two types of environments, cypress-tupelo gum growing in wet places, and varieties of oaks, hickories, elms and other trees collectively called bottomland hardwoods on slightly higher floodplain levels. Both are annually inundated in winter and spring. These floodplain forests and river corridors are the refuge, feeding grounds and pathways for a host of wildlife including deer, bear, cougar and otter, plus numerous birds such as the rare limpkin and swallowtail kite, and an array of reptiles. Old river channels and even inundated floodplains are the spawning grounds of marine fish such as sturgeon, striped bass and three species of shad, providing an opportunity for excellent fishing. One such Oxbow Lake in Telfair County produced the world's record largemouth bass.

Within 20 miles of the coast the rivers enter the influence of the tides. Our knowledge of these tidewater forests is limited, but cypress grow huge here as do the tupelo and other gum trees. We know because we have a virgin stand of gum-cypress in the center of the 6,000 acre Lewis Island tract recently purchased by the state, and which may form part of a huge river park embracing the lower Altamaha. Some of the Lewis Island giants are estimated to be 1200 years old, standing approximately 1100 feet back from the channels, about the maximum length of cable used by early loggers from barge-mounted winches. Another type of virgin cypress forest occurs in narrow, deep, lake-like channels of tributaries to the larger rivers such as Savannah's Ebenezer Creek in Effingham County. Having a diameter that is hardly large enough to attract loggers, these trees have fantastic swollen bases, some so wide that a person can sit upon them. They are best observed in summer and fall during low water, enhancing one of the most beautiful boat rides in the state.

Waters which disappear into the great limestone aquifer in the upper Coastal Plain later emerge as springs and sometimes streams. This is especially true along Spring Creek in Decatur

County. The larger springs are a little ways from the stream, such as the beautiful Brinson Springs. Spring Creek, in the summer and fall, is a spectacular canoe ride, for the crystal clear water reveals a limestone rock bottom, with abundant clams and schools of golden shad that dart by.

Some limesinks feed the deep aquifer, being circular basins caused by collapse of underground caverns, and are either dry or filled with water. They occur largely around Valdosta and in the southwest, west of the Pelham Escarpment which divides the limesink region from the vast middle Coastal Plain called the "Tifton Plateau". This escarpment, into which the *torreya ravines* are incised near the Florida line, has some fascinating deep limesinks, some connected with an extensive underground cave system. West of the Pelham Escarpment, which parallels the Flint River, most streams are underground and fields are shaped by man; eastward the fields are shaped by the million tiny tributaries of surface streams.

Thick sands overlying the limestone aquifer that lies deep beneath south Georgia are the source of water which produces the second major type of Coastal Plain stream, the blackwater river, whose waters are stained dark by the acid gum and cypress swamps of innumerable tributaries. The blackwater rivers make exciting canoe trails and the gleaming white sand bars make excellent camping places. The Alapaha is a noted canoe trail and is reputed to be one of the state's purest streams with only occasional limestone shoals to interrupt the dark water. Blackwater stream levels drop low in the late fall—thus the ideal float trip is made during summer or early autumn. Although aquatic life may not be as abundant as in the larger alluvial rivers, blackwater streams abound with fat bluegill and redbreast bream which vacuum-clean the numerous underwater snags of swarming aquatic insect larvae.

As we reach the Fall Line, and gradually drop off into the Coastal Plain, we cross several zones where the soils and vegetation differ. The first Coastal Plain zone is known officially as the Fall Line Sand Hills. This zone, deposited during the Cretaceous portion of the Age of Dinosaurs, contains immense sandhills especially in its western and eastern parts. It also contains numerous kaolin clay mines which make Georgia the top industrial clay producer in the world. It is here in Talbot and Taylor Counties we first meet the remarkable sandhill community forested with dwarf oaks, called turkey oaks, over which originally towered longleaf pine. This hot, arid sandy terrain supports a combination of plants and animals thought to be extremely old. These plants and animals are adapted to the aridity of the sands, which also protects them from fire when the environment occasionally burns. Almost all animal life is burrowing; the pocket gopher, a squirrel-sized mammal makes a series of mounds with no openings, while the other prominent denizen, the gopher turtle, makes a long deep hole with a large turtle-shaped entrance hole and low sand mound in front. The gopher turtle burrow supports a unique assortment of insects and vertebrates including the gopher frog, the diamond back rattler and the endangered indigo snake which share the turtle's home, especially as a winter retreat.

The gopher turtle and the turkey oak populate other sandhills farther south. The most intriguing of these are parabolic-shaped sandhills lying east of the Ohoopee and Canoochee Rivers. While many Georgia streams have sandhills only on the eastern side, the curious "Ohoopee dunes" as they are called, are the most outstanding. State geologists first noted these unusual dunes in looking at satellite images. The dunes, presumed to be of wind origin during the Pleistocene, are up to five miles long and several miles wide. They bear the characteristic longleaf pine-turkey oak community, yet with the addition of some evergreen shrubs—one, rosemary, is dark green and resembles a squat cedar. Two woody mints which bear red or purple flowers are much more common than the rosemary. Some of the riverine dunes bear hammocks dominated by evergreen live and laurel oaks and, occasionally, one finds an enchanted forest of dwarfed live oaks naturally bonsaid, with the sands carpeted with a weird abundance of lichens.

Often in the sand hills and less commonly over much of the central plateau of Georgia, one finds cypress ponds, or small sphagnum-filled bogs occupied by shrubs and more interestingly, sweet and loblolly bays, both with beautiful large flowers. The latter closely resembles the bay-like tree *Franklinia alatamaha*, which the Bartrams found in bay swamps along the Altamaha River at Fort Barrington, but which has never been found since the early years of exploration.

The Fall Line sandhills are quite old, perhaps 90 million years, the river dunes are thought to be of ice age origin, formed perhaps 1 million years ago. The coastal dunes are more recent. There are two sets of these dunes on many of the coastal islands; recent dunes just back of the present beach, and another older or Silver Bluff series farther back. Cumberland and Jekyll show both sets, other islands like Wassaw and Blackbeard and Little St. Simons are very young and usually have rolling, though forested younger dune surfaces. The interior of most islands is flatter and more stable terrain. Back of the Silver Bluff dunes almost all the islands are forested with a mixture of pines and evergreen oaks. Of the latter two, the live oak is dominant being a truly remarkable tree as well as the state tree. Reaching great age it has almost no trunk and its huge limbs sprawl and twist and are, of course, draped with Spanish moss. Salt tolerant, wind-pruned examples are able to grow on the back of the rear dune systems and help stabilize the shifting, flowing sand. The front dunes and interdune areas are stabilized by sea oats, water-penny and a variety of other plants and vines. Sand dunes anywhere cannot take much punishment from hooves, tires or feet—vegetation precariously anchors the dunes which, on abuse, tend to advance inward and bury the forest. If the live oaks are not inundated by sand they may be undermined by wave erosion. Most coastal islands are eroding on the north end. On Wassaw, the bleached skeletons of live oak adorn the beaches.

One Coastal Plain environment even drier than the sandhills is the sandstone outcrops which stretch as a belt across the central Coastal Plain. Where no shoals were created when the Oconee and Ocmulgee crossed these sandstone ledges, great weirs often were constructed to deepen the current so that river boats could pass. Near Broxton in Coffee County is a remarkable gorge some 20 to 30 feet deep eroded into sandstone with deep crevices and caves. It is called "The Rocks". It has never been fully explored.

The coastal islands are parts of the Pliocene-Pleistocene sea floor. The flat sea floor here was covered by at least four successive inundations and extends 40 to 50 miles inland. We can delineate it by drawing a line from the Screven-Effingham County line to the Tattnall-Long County boundary, down the Altamaha ten miles thence southwest to meeting place of Pierce, Ware and Brantley Counties. Seaward of this line the highways are arrow straight and the forest is an endless tree farm called *pine flatwoods*. Originally much of this area was covered with slow-growing longleaf pine, with slash pine confined to the very wettest, lowest terrain (only a foot or so of elevation will make a difference). With the cutting of the longleaf, the faster-growing slash has been encouraged wherever pines grow. The understory is a thick tangle of a dwarf palm called *palmetto* and a variety of heath plants, predominated by gallberry holly, the source of excellent honey. Original longleaf pine older than 200 years can be seen on several plantations, such as Greenwood, near Thomasville. Although longleaf does not reach the size of the commonest Piedmont pine, loblolly, a forest of old longleafs is impressive. The longleaf pine is remarkably fire-adapted. Its bark is not only resistant but the terminal bud of the young seedlings is protected from fire damage by a plume of long, dense needles. In fact the pinelands contain many fire-adapted species.

So important is fire management to the health of both pine forests and their wildlife that Tall Timbers Research Station near Thomasville is devoted to the effects of fire in natural environments. Apparently lightning-caused fires were rampant before man arrived from Asia over 20,000 years ago. There is reasonable evidence that the great mammoths and other Pleistocene fauna trudged through the colonnades of the great southern pine forests up until perhaps 10,000 years ago. Their teeth and bones are common in the springs and springfed streams along the Georgia-Florida boundary. If fire is kept out, as experiments at Tall Timber prove, a hardwood forest will eventually replace the pine forest. It is for this reason that ecologists apply the terms "fire-climax" or "pre-climax" to the southern pine forests. Fire obviously keeps hardwood seedlings suppressed.

Fire is necessary for the maintenance of another picturesque Coastal Plain environment, the famous *pitcher plant bog,* which is an opening in the pine forests dominated by herbs of which the erect trumpets of several species of insect-eating pitcher plants are characteristic. These bogs are low in nitrogen and apparently insect-eating plants do well there. The sundews with their sticky threads and gobs, also catch insects and are common. These bog meadows contain the southern area's most spectacular display of flowers during spring and summer.

The best known bog in Georgia is the Okefenokee Swamp which extends slightly into Florida. This giant peat-filled basin has very acid water and is approximately 12 feet deep. Actually the Okefenokee is a mosaic of several types of environments. There are narrow lakes, cypress forests, and islands supporting pines and some oak hammock. And then there are the prairies, open water but covered with emergent grasses, orchids, pickeral weed and water lilies. This is the home of Allan's water rat or *Neofiber,* a miniature copy of a muskrat for there are no true muskrats in south Georgia. Allan's rat builds its little conical grass lodges in grassy areas of the priarie. The Okefenokee is more a frog heaven than a snake paradise for actually, few snakes are seen. Two giant eel-like salamanders, Siren and Amphiuma, are common here, although they also occur in Coastal Plain River swamps. Both reach a length of over three feet and a weight of several pounds thus rivaling the hellbender of the Tennessee drainage as America's largest salamander. The Okefenokee, like many cypress ponds and other wetland environments in the Coastal Plain, actually burns at times, on an interval of 20 to 30 years. The brownish plant residue, or peat, reaches quite close

Pages 24 and 25: East of the State's great rivers are obscure fairylands called evergreen/scrub-lichen forest. A rare environment filled with three species of lichens, such as reindeer moss, a primitive lycopod, and capped with dwarfed live oaks of great age. Ohoopee Sand Hills, Highway Number 1, Emanuel County.

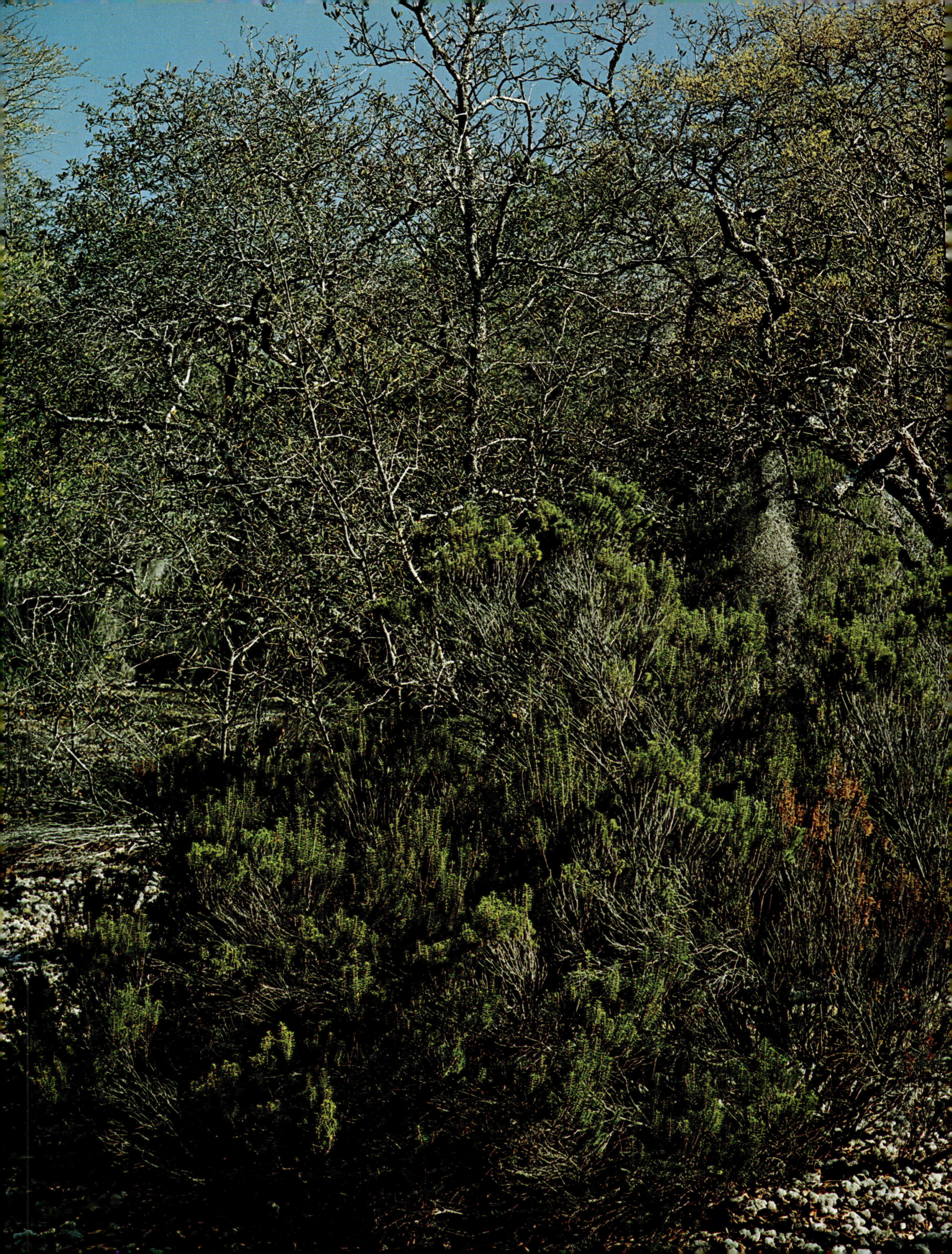

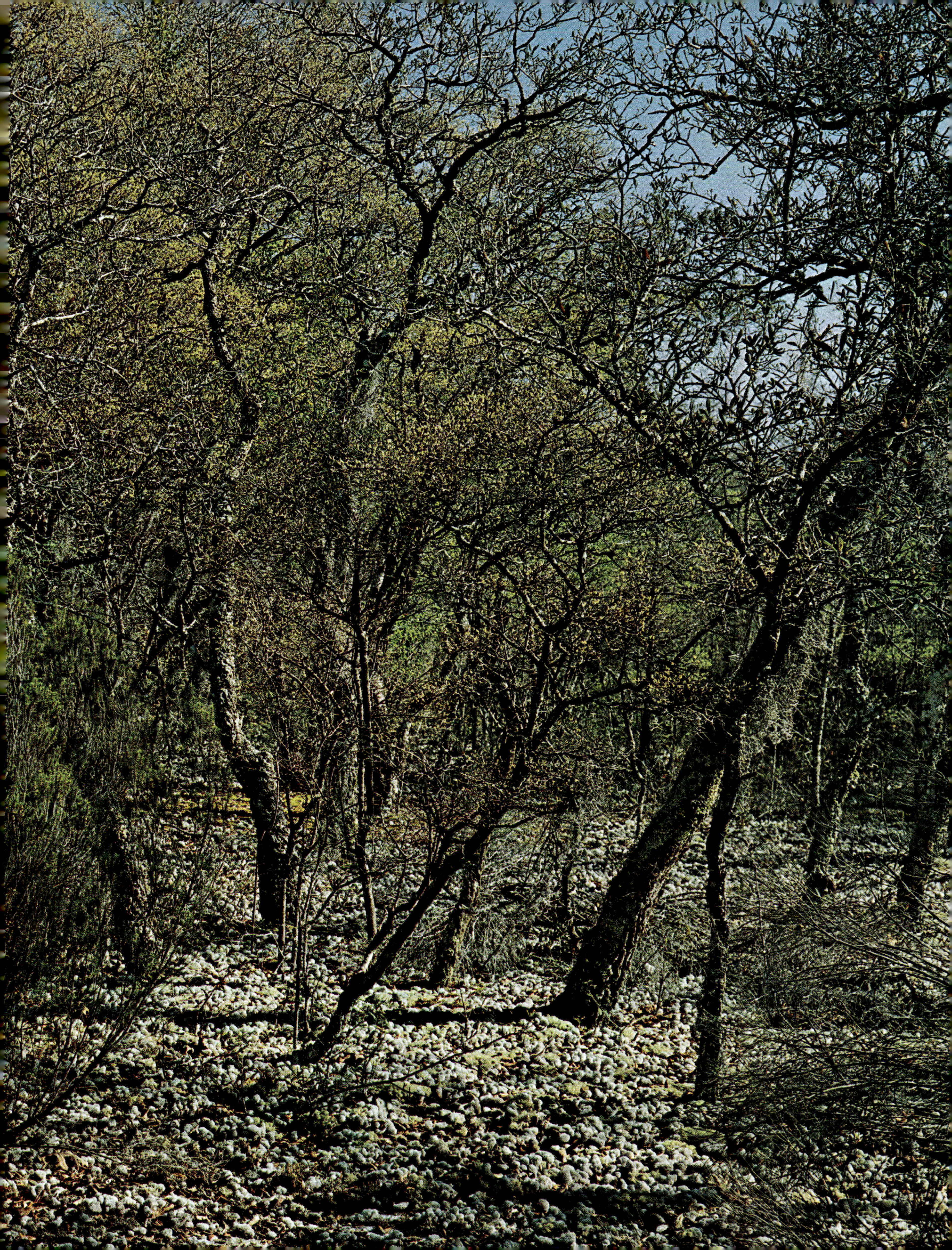

to the surface, and is burned out periodically, along with encroaching cypress seedlings. Thus the open prairies are maintained. The Okefenokee is drained by the Suwanee and the St. Marys Rivers. Now that it is a wilderness area, canoe trips into and across it on water trails, provide unique experiences. Camping platforms have been erected and away from these, the water is normally pure enough to drink. The swamp is entered at three major points; a state park at Billy's Lake near Fargo, an old logging canal at Camp Cornelia near Folkston and Kingfisher Landing near Racepond on U.S. Highway 1. At Kingfisher there is a series of canals excavated during a now-abandoned attempt to market Okefenokee peat commercially. Okefenokee Swamp Park near Waycross provides swamp lore and a look at characteristic animal life.

ORIGIN OF THE LANDFORM

No other southeastern state includes such a diversity of geologic landforms, stretching from the Cumberland Plateau in the extreme northwest across Appalachia and the Piedmont to the offshore coastal islands the type of which, incidentally, are found elsewhere only along a portion of the South Carolina coast.

Natural environments are first of all determined by the geology of the land. A capsule version of how our state got to look that way will increase our appreciation of how nature and man have used the basic resources of the state. We will begin in the extreme northwest and pass eastward and southward.

By 300 million years ago the vast inland seas that had covered most of our state had shrunk to a trough which led diagonally northeastward through the northern half. This great trough (Applachian geosyncline) led from Alabama to Pennsylvania. Filled with up to six miles of sediments the earth's crust was depressed. Pressure from the viscous mantle of the earth's rocks began to buckle and overlap these sediments resulting in folds oriented from southwest to northeast. In places the rocks cracked at fault lines, causing some to slide up higher than others. Constant erosion over millions of years wore away over two miles of soft rock and some of the folds containing harder rocks such as sandstone formed ridges during this process. Or sometimes, a sandstone layer would be thrust to the surface by a thrust fault. This is the origin of the Armuchee Ridges which border the west side of the Great Valley in the extreme northwest area. Farther westward, the folds of Lookout and Sand Mountains were subject to less pressure and the beds are flatter. Sandstone caps form the tops of these plateaus, which comprise the eastern edge of the Cumberland Plateau of Tennessee, where the sedimentary beds are nearly horizontal.

The eastern edge of the sedimentary beds of the northwest are sharply marked by one of the earth's great faults. Known as the Great Smoky Fault near Cartersville along U.S. Highway 411, it clearly separates the unmodified fossiliferous rocks of the northwest from non-fossil bearing rocks of the Cohuttas lying to the east which are clearly sediments modified by heat and pressure but containing strata very much like slates linking them with the inland sea.

Although the Cohuttas, lying just east of U.S. Highway 411, strongly show their sedimentary heritage, there is a marked difference in all the mountains to the east of the Great Smoky Fault. They are not long ridges, alternating with long, linear valleys, but eroded into rounded peaks arranged with little discernable pattern. There is a pattern in the earth's surface however, that divides the Cohuttas from the Blue Ridge proper. So very obvious from Land Satellite imagery this narrow trough, the Murphy Syncline, stretches from Jasper through Ellijay and Blue Ridge and is the obvious route for a new U.S. Highway 400. Currently U.S. Highway 76 and State Highway 5 follow this natural pathway. East of the Murphy Syncline lie the Piedmont and Blue Ridge both composed of the same rock type and obviously subjected to enormous pressure and heat because the minerals composing the original sediments appear as crystals, making a very distinct and often harder rock. Where did the pressure come from? Current geologic theory holds that this force came from the southeast and resulted from the collision of the African and North American continents presumably about 200 million years ago during upper Permian Age. The two continents, plus South America, tore apart and began the voyage to their present positions somewhat later. There are other shear zones that may have resulted from this collision with Africa; one being the Brevard Fault which the Chattahoochee River follows faithfully southwestward across the entire Georgia Piedmont. Here, long parallel ridges are capped with erosion-resistant quartzite or metamorphosed sandstone.

Tallulah Gorge is cut in another large quartzite deposit in northeast Georgia, forming yet another geologic event that is one of the most remarkable examples of stream capture in the world. Originally the Chattooga and Tallulah Rivers were the headwaters of the Chattahoochee, but since the Savannah was cutting down faster, one of its tributaries cut through the water divide and captured the Chattahoochee headwaters.

This leads us to the best explanation for the difference in elevation between the Blue Ridge and Piedmont, since the rock structure is the same. Streams such as the Savannah have a shorter distance to travel before their entry into the Atlantic than do the Tennessee tributaries. Hence the stream with the shortest distance to go drops the fastest and cuts downward more, thus the Piedmont is simply being base leveled faster.

The actual mineral structure of the rock may produce mountains locally. For example the micas in rocks called schists resist weathering more than the feldspars in harder rocks. Some lesser terrain features are also the result of physical weathering. During the last ice age which ended approximately 10,000 years ago, freeze-thaw cycles created unique boulderfields of ice-mined rocks on the north faces of some of our highest peaks such as Brasstown Bald, Tray and Hightower, as well as in the Cohuttas and Rich Mountain area. Also, gravity-tumbled rocks and eroded soil filled mountain valleys with deposits of colluvium creating flat zones resembling flood plains.

During the Wisconsin ice age between about 14,000 and 20,000 years ago the steep mountain slopes were covered with conifer forests, which probably burned with catastrophic results. Erosion of undreamed magnitude may have occurred on the naked slopes following fires, especially with epic rainstorm events as the 1000 year flood or hurricanes. There is evidence that, with the retreat of the polar ice between 10,000 and 18,000 years ago wind cycles changed and the southeast was subject to a wet period when streams carried considerably more sediment. Increased river flow during glacial and post glacial events may have contributed heavily to the formation of existing floodplains of both the Piedmont and Coastal Plains.

Some scientists believe that powerful winds from the southwest during the last glacial period are responsible for the sand hills on the eastern side of many Georgia Coastal Plain streams. These winds are believed by some to also explain the origin of the remarkable, shallow, oval pits called Carolina Bays, over 1000 of which have been located in the lower Coastal Plain of Georgia and whose axis is usually northwest to southeast, or at right angles to strong southwest winds of glacial times. An appealing alternative explanation of their origin is that they were formed by showers of non-metallic meteorites.

Pine Mountain is an unusual long ridge in the southern Piedmont identifiable because it is capped with resistant quartzites and mica schists. In Bartow, Cherokee and Pickens counties are other low ridges that are capped with quartzite, similar to Pine Mountain; the most predominant being Pine Log Mountain. Elsewhere in the Piedmont there are bumps, knobs and ridges of an entirely different origin, formed from molten igneous rock, injected upward into the metamorphosed sediments which make up the bulk of the Piedmont.

These ingenous rocks are of several types with Soapstone Ridge southeast of Atlanta crossed by Interstate 285, being one crystallized from a magma rich in iron and magnesium. The so-called granite outcrops are other types, formed from rocks rich in silica and aluminum. The rounded domes of Panola in Henry County and Stone Mountain in DeKalb County are individually composed of different kinds of granites. Mount Arabia, while also considered a granite outcrop is yet composed of another type of rock where the light bands are of igneous and the dark bands are of metamorphosed sediments. Because of these immense bedrock exposures, the state has become the world's major producer of granite products.

The Coastal Plain begins at the Fall Line, running through the cities of Augusta, Macon and Columbus. One discerns this boundary with difficulty while driving, because the deep red soils of the Piedmont weather very similarly to the soils of the upper Coastal Plain, all merging to form gently rolling hills. It is the character of the rivers which changes with startling suddenness at the Fall Line. Because the great rivers of Georgia namely the Oconee, Ocmulgee, Flint and Savannah have incised more rapidly into the somewhat softer, flatter Coastal Plain, they form vast swamps up to four miles wide, immediately on leaving the hard rocks of their Piedmont beds. Slowed down, the rivers can carry less sediment and thus form wide floodplains. Except for an occasional sandstone outcrop, they are seldom again troubled by hard bedrock.

The entire Coastal Plain is composed of nearly flat layers of sediments recently uplifted from the sea floor. Sharks teeth, whale bones and marine shells occur in profusion in bedrock sandstones and limestones all across the Coastal Plain. The innermost belt of sediments lapped against the Fall Line is the Cretaceous, the last epoch of the Age of Dinosaurs. It is composed of immense deposits of marine sands and clays, some of which are called kaolin. The Cretaceous seas were the greatest inundation of all time; some geologists feel that they inundated a good portion of the Piedmont itself. The later seas of the dawn of the Age of Mammals deposited sediments on top of the Cretaceous sea floor; their sediments comprise other bands across the upper Coastal Plain. These shallow Eocene and Paleocene seas left a large portion of the southwest areas west of Cordele, Albany and Bainbridge covered with a limestone which is very close to the surface, containing many caverns for the free flow of underground streams. The rest of central Coastal Plain is composed of the sands, sandstones and clays from the Miocene and Pliocene sea floors.

The lower Coastal Plain, usually within 60 miles of the present ocean edge, is called the Plio-Pleistocene. It is quite young, being 3 million years of age, and reasonably flat. During the Pleistocene, the repeated thawing and freezing of huge polar ice caps alternately raised and lowered sea levels around the world. Thus the ocean edge staged a series of advances, depositing largely sands on top of the old Miocene sediments. On its retreat the sea edge would often move many miles seaward of the present shore, exposing large areas and forming barrier islands on the Continental Shelf. During the last ice age, the Wisconsin of 20,000 years ago, the ocean front lay at least 50 miles off the present shore. Inland, there are at least six sets of old beaches and dunes running parallel with the present coastline. The most remarkable of these is the north-south trending Trail Ridge which trapped an old shallow arm of the sea forming what is now a fresh water basin, called Okefenokee. It is noted for an abundance of plant, animal, and birdlife.

Some of our golden isles such as Cumberland and Jekyll present two dune systems with a broad interdune area. The dunes nearest the sea are recent, the second set way back may be much older, of Silver Bluff age. The oldest, the Silver Bluff, was formed when the sea stood about five feet higher, 30,000 years ago. The level interior of the present-day barrier islands is then relatively old. Other islands like Wassaw may be entirely covered with recent dunes, their surfaces are rolling and not flat. The present mainland shore bears an older set of barrier islands, the Princess Anne, formed when the sea stood about 15 feet higher than present. On the mainland the sea floor is very flat and low—highways must be built up from fill dredged from shallow ditches on each side, providing homes for aquatic plants and animals including alligators. Occasionally the highway rises over old beach and dune lines and back of them on slightly higher ground, pine flatwoods and cypress swamps stand in what was likely former salt marshes or lagoons behind ancient barrier islands.

Strong currents and diagonal wave action rapidly change the offshore islands. The north ends erode and the sand is deposited at the south end. Sometimes new islands are formed. Williamson Island just south of Little Tybee has grown in 40 years from zero to 10,000 feet in length!

Thus Georgia presents a spectrum of geologic history which stretches from the first dawn of life in shallow marine seas 500 million years ago to the emergence of new coastal islands within two decades. It is all presided over and humbled in age by the great backbone of the Appalachians, which is one of the world's oldest mountain masses.

ORIGIN OF THE LIFEFORMS

Though inanimate forces of geologic upheaval and erosion by water and wind roughly shape the landform, it is also modified by plants and animals, who take advantage of the niches made available by the raw materials of water, slope and bedrock under the prevailing climate. In fact one of the attributes of natural environments is that the living members try to minimize the destruction of the land form by physical forces and thus preserve their own habitat. This cooperation for survival by animate and inanimate participants leads to our concept of natural units, or ecosystems, which tend to be stable for long periods of time. The ultimately stable unit in the Piedmont is the oak-hickory forest ecosystem. But since geologic time is immeasurably long and climate changes, the state has not always looked the way it does today. We have scarcely enough data to do more than glimpse the broad picture during and since the last great ice age.

About 20,000 years ago a great, miles thick, wall of ice stood over the northern United States. The water locked inside sank the world's oceans 300 feet and Georgia's Coastal Plain extended flatly out at least 50 miles. Continental wind patterns changed to a dry cold climate, causing most of the region to appear as does present-day Quebec, 1400 miles to the north at 48 north latitude. The Appalachian's highest peak, 6,684-foot Mt. Mitchell, was likely capped with moss-lichen tundra down to 4500 feet. A vast black forest of spruce and fir covered much of the Appalachians and probably capped the state's higher peaks. Most mountain slopes and the Piedmont were probably covered with jack and red pine, including a few deciduous trees, largely oaks, hanging on in moist coves. Boreal or northern forest animals, largely vegetarian, mouse-like creatures such as red-backed voles, ranged as far south as northern Florida. Spruce grouse, gray jays and other Canadian birds were common. Summer temperatures may have averaged 30 degrees, winter temperatures near zero degrees Fahrenheit. Aquatic salamanders and fish were able to survive the intense cold, everything else had to live underground, hibernate, store up food or migrate to warmer climes. Most of the small mammals had to be either vegetarians like the voles, or be able to exist on a diet of spruce-fir seeds, like the red squirrel.

At this time it is thought that part of the great Pleistocene megafauna of mammoths and bison had lumbered across the dry Bering Strait from Asia followed by man. Other, such as the giant ground sloth and glyptodont, arrived from South America. Evidence suggests that with the advent of stone-tipped projectiles such as spears and arrows and the use of fire-drives, the great beasts were eventually destroyed by man. Because Florida and the great off shore flatlands offered the warmest and best feeding grounds, it is here that the great ice age beasts last lived to meet their demise approximately 10,000 years ago, at the close of the ice age after man had arrived in this area. Many were apparently driven into the blackwater rivers and spring runs of northern Florida and perhaps southern Georgia. Since the clear waters from the great underground Eocene aquifer carried no silt to cover them, the teeth and bones of these great shaggy creatures often carpeted the bottom of springs and the clear runs issuing from them.

About 10,000 years ago, as it warmed and moisture increased, a deciduous forest of beech, oak and hickory began to reclaim the pine-dominated slopes of the mountains and perhaps the Piedmont as well. About 5000 years ago, longleaf pine forests began to replace the dry oak scrub and savannah in the southern area and rising water tables led to vast cypress swamps and ponds. Essentially modern environments were thought to be evident about 4000 years ago. Some communities, already dry-adapted, such as those on high unchanging sand hills of the Cretaceous, were perhaps there all along, having persisted as long as 30 million years.

With the close of the ice age 10,000 years ago terrestrial, cold-adapted flora and fauna became extinct. Some Pleistocene relicts are able to survive now in our mountains only at the highest elevations or in deep ravines. The red-backed vole barely enters the state at 2500 feet down a steep, cold gorge on the Tallulah River, and on the top of Rabun Bald.

The cold-adapted salamanders remained in their Appalachian stronghold. In fact, there are 38 species there, making this region number one in the world. Other lesser known creatures have proliferated and spread into our area as have the salamanders. The Appalachians have been a center of origin for snails for a long time, there being 167 kinds in the southern Appalachians alone! This area is also the global center for millipedes, a cousin of the centipede, where 234 species have been described and an estimated 250 more undescribed.

In addition to those animals that invaded Georgia from the mountains a few forms have come from the west, but the other major routes were either down the Coastal Plain from the north or reinvasion from Florida and the now submerged refuge lands on the Continental Shelf. Two of the latter animals were the cottonmouth and alligator. In warmer pre-glacial times when palm trees grew in Alaska the ancestral cottonmouth migrated from Asia where its cousins are legion. It is at this time that the alligator was both here and on the Asiatic Pacific coast. In fact, the Southeast probably shares more plants and animals with China than with any other part of the world, except Europe. For another example, our giant salamander, the hellbender, found in Georgia rivers such as the Toccoa, Little Tennessee, and Hiawassee, has close relatives in the rivers of China.

Our fauna then, either survived the cold, dry conditions of the ice age by being already adapted to cold, dryness or, coincidentally fire, or it reinvaded Georgia as modern plant communities were reestablished. Having initially noted the interaction of prehistoric man and mastodon in Southern Georgia we need to review man's participation as a new animal component of the post-Pleistocene ecosystems of the state.

MAN AND THE GEORGIA ECOSYSTEMS

Given the encounter of geologic and climatic forces on natural systems of rock, soil and fauna, the story of our environments would be incomplete without considering the impact of man, the ultimate consumer, as a new participant in the ecosystem. In spite of nature's built-in resiliency, it has been a strain to accommodate her latest child. Man has exploited to the fullest the natural wealth he found in this state. In the case of the American Indians their numbers were small and their impact minimal, yet the earliest explorers document a remarkable number of fields, clearings and burned forests. We are presumptuous to conclude that the Indians were the first conservationists. They, like those who displaced them, took of nature's bounty as they could, in the easiest way possible. There was one essential and distinct difference, the Indians did not claim land for individual aggrandizement.

In reviewing the awesome speed of man's domination over natural communities, one wonders how any natural beauty remains, even within a state blessed with original wealth of soil and forest. America was a teeming gameland 25,000 years ago when man first spread out over the continent. The roots of man in North America go back even further, for he came from Siberia, perhaps as early as 35,000 years ago, following herds of caribou and bison and mammoth. Eventually, he found an ice-free corridor southward from Alaska onto the great plains. Man was only one of many animal migrants from Asia. On his arrival he found an Asiatic fauna of muskox, yak, bison, moose, lion, horse, mammoth, grizzly, deer, otter, skunk and copperhead snake. Other animals, like the grotesque ground sloths, the opossum, armadillo, porcupine and coral snake, had arrived from South America. A far lesser number originated here: camels, wolf, cougar and mastodon.

The latest marked changes in this region's environment began with the abrupt decimation of the ice-age forests between 11,000 and 14,000 years ago. About 11,000 years ago man first arrived here and began to change his environment with the abrupt extinction of the great ice-age mammals such as the mammoth and mastodon. How frequently he used fire to drive the huge beasts to their demise is conjectural. Lightning-caused fire was probably already preventing much of south Georgia from becoming hardwood forest when man arrived.

These early hunters of the large beasts we call Paleo-Indians whose culture reached its peak in 9000 B.C., then evolved into organized hunter-gatherers of the Archaic Period (8000-500 B.C.) and who reached their pinnacle about 5000 years ago. The Archaic groups foraged smaller animals, plants and fish and inhabited Georgia until 500 B.C. During the following Woodland Period, occurring between 500 B.C. and A.D. 1000, man became even more settled—Georgia rivers such as the Flint and Etowah still bear underwater the long converging stone weirs which funneled fish into nets or traps. Prior to the Woodland Period's clay vessels, Indian cultures quarried pots from soft rock outcrops such as DeKalb County's Soapstone Ridge, occupied rock shelters along Georgia streams and created shell mounds on the coastal islands.

It is said that natural environments determined Indian culture more than location, chronology or tradition. Beginning about 3000 B.C. the harvesting economy made intensive use of the commonest local foods such as deer, acorns, clams and fish. In turn, man more and more began to modify the landscape. About 1000 A.D. the Mississippian Period began, during which time Indians in Georgia continued the horticulture of the late Woodland Period, replanting useful plants and scattering seeds. By 1200 A.D. corn-bean-squash agriculture was in full swing and DeSoto, who entered Georgia in 1540, chronicled vast cornfields stretching to the horizon.

The Mississippian Indians built enormous earth mounds, some exceeding in basal area the great pyramid of Egypt. The mounds at Macon and Etowah are on or near the floodplains where corn was grown in rich alluvial soil renewed periodically by natural inundation. As did some early Caucasian settlers, the Indians ringed the bark of trees and left the dead trees standing. Upland soils, unlike bottomlands, are not periodically renewed by silt deposition but must be made fertile by hundreds of years of plants and animals living undisturbed on their surface, concentrating the stuff of life in thin, dark layers. So, as fertility waned in upland fields, Indians simply shifted to new forest areas. In certain environments, Indian fire, following abandonment of fields favored the growth of rank river cane. Enormous areas of cane prevailed, according to William Bartram. Vestiges of this river cane may still be seen in the river swamps.

In earliest historical records, Georgia was a mosaic of Indian tribes, among them the Uchees and Yamacraws on the Savannah, the Hitchiti and Cowetas on the Ocmulgee, the Oconees on the Oconee, the Chehaws and Oswichees on the Flint and Chattahoochee and the Cherokees in the mountains. All of these smaller tribes, except the widespread Cherokee, were soon amalgamated by the invading Alabama Muscogees into the powerful Creek Confederacy.

Caucasian man first occupied the Georgia coastal islands and the coastal strip of land immediately shoreward. The northern half of Coastal Georgia was long called the "debatable land" and claimed by Spanish, French and English explorers. But the British won and with the first yielding of tidewater lands to Oglethorpe by the Yamacraw chief Tomochichi, the Caucasian settlements of Georgia began inexorbly to swallow the Creek Nation strip by strip in the following sequence: a strip between the Ogeechee and Savannah Rivers (1773); westward to the Oconee (1784), westward to the Ocmulgee as far north as the Ulcoufauhatchee, being the present-day Alcovy (1805), the extreme southern counties next to Florida (1814), the area south of the Ocmulgee's Big Bend (1818), west to the Flint River (1821), and finally west to the Alabama line (1825). As the frontier advanced, many of the Indians deserted organized agriculture and reverted to hunting and gathering, bringing into being an ample supply of deerskins and other trade items. By 1820 white civilization had covered Georgia.

During these early years, the major rivers were the lifeblood of Georgia's interior. Shallow-draft boats called "pole boats", laboriously poled by 12 men, were a fragile life with the coast. The vast forests of slow-growing longleaf pine that had amazed early explorers went down river in enormous log rafts to Darien, which became the lumber export capital of the New World. The great "yellow" pine forests were virtually gone by 1895.

A highway network with stagecoaches covered early Georgia and in 1816 steamboats appeared on the Savannah and two years later on the Altamaha. The first run up to Ocmulgee to the new inland city of Macon began in 1829. Over 200 of these craft eventually plied the Chattahoochee-Flint system. Steamboats towing barges could tote a variety of farm products, and agriculture intensified, especially for the magic, hollow fiber of cotton, leading to the plantation system and the Ante-Bellum era. Plantations had the advantage of massive organized labor that could fell upland forests as well as the cathedral forests of gum-cypress to make way for ricefields. Rice became a coastal staple as early as 1770 and, with the creation of the tidal-flooding method in South Carolina in 1750, reached its zenith in Georgia in 1860.

Unlike the Indian the white settlers had no virgin forests nearby to deaden when the old soil was depleted of the accumulated wealth of centuries. And since the environments were designed for forest cover, soils were vulnerable to row crop agriculture and heavy rains eroded them. As early as 1850 wagon-loads of settlers set out for the "new" soils of Alabama and Mississippi.

Soil exploitation intensified rapidly. Following the invention of the cotton gin in 1793 there followed two peaks of cotton monoculture, one using the residual fertility of the remaining topsoil, the other sustained by the availability of Chilean nitrate as fertilizer. The end product was the loss of almost all remaining Piedmont topsoil. Piedmont lands were eventually abandoned in three phases: during and following the Civil War, during the agricultural depression of the 1880's and following the boll weevil of the 1920's. The Piedmont passed back into secondary forest. This secondary forest was itself exploited three times: lightly until 1920, severely during World War II and after, and steadily by pulpwood harvest since the mid-1940's.

Almost all of the virgin cathedral forest of cypress that had awed William Bartram had been floated out by the 1930's, the Okefenokee was cut by 1926. The vast pinelands were acquired for paper cellulose products and industrial forests of fast-growing slash pine supplanted the old longleaf pine-wiregrass community which, along with the wetlands, had sustained the bison and perhaps even the mammoth in earlier times.

Almost simultaneously the virgin mountain hardwood forests vanished and the United States purchased these cut-over lands as the nucleus of the Cherokee and later, Chattahoochee National Forests. The earliest mountain pioneers subsisted with a cornpatch, garden and cattle and hogs fed without cost on the rich nuts of the oak-chestnut forests. Later forest and mineral exploitation began in earnest. As the timber was exhausted and the native abrasive corundum ore lost place to electrically fused aluminum oxide, and mica gave way to glass, the pioneers largely withdrew from the mountain country which rapidly became wild once more. Then the mountain lion once again roamed into the northern regions and under Forest Service custodianship the forest regrew, the slopes undepleted of valuable topsoil.

Thus it is that the mountains recovered their forests, shielding within steep and rough places the state's last virgin old-growth timber. Some Piedmont bluffs, too steep for cotton, escaped the advance of the loblolly or "old field" pine. And Coastal Plain swamps and many wetland ponds recovered much of their visual glory. Only the expert can tell the slash pine forest today from the longleaf predecessor of yesteryear. Thus it is that Georgia's landforms yet conceal vistas of charm and wildness for those who would seek them out.

Very recently, throughout the southeast, man has endorsed modifications of environments that may change forever their structure and function. Clearcutting in the mountains and river swamps, channelization of streams and the bulldozing of dwarf oak forests on the sand hills are examples that more and more greet the quizzical eye of the traveller.

Perhaps, if the vital life support functions of river swamp, mountain slope forest and other natural ecosystems can soon be understood and if accepted along with their charm and wildness, they can yet inspire and sustain the generations of tomorrow.

Dukes Creek tumbles fluidly out of a golden
light-fringed forest in Raven Cliffs Scenic Area,
Richard Russell Scenic Highway.

An abstract maze of rare orange lichen clings
to a boulder at the bottom of the
Tallulah Gorge.

The gentle flow of water casually arranged
this leaf/needle embrace. Dukes Creek Falls
along Richard Russell Scenic Highway.

Beneath Toccoa Falls, a prism canopy of truth
soaks every fiber of life.

A million leaves radiate their flavor in one last explosion of love for the world. Georgia/North Carolina border, on State Highway Number 246.

This colossal hemlock stands as a reminder of the awesome and pristine forests that once covered most of North Georgia. A special place to pause and meditate, Patterson's Gap, Clayton.

Rime-covered oaks proclaim the arrival of an early winter. This matrix of seasons transpired on top of highest point in Georgia, 4,784 foot Brasstown Bald. Pages 40 and 41: Late evening light smoothingly skims the mountains that overlook Hiawassee Lake. View looking west from Brasstown Bald.

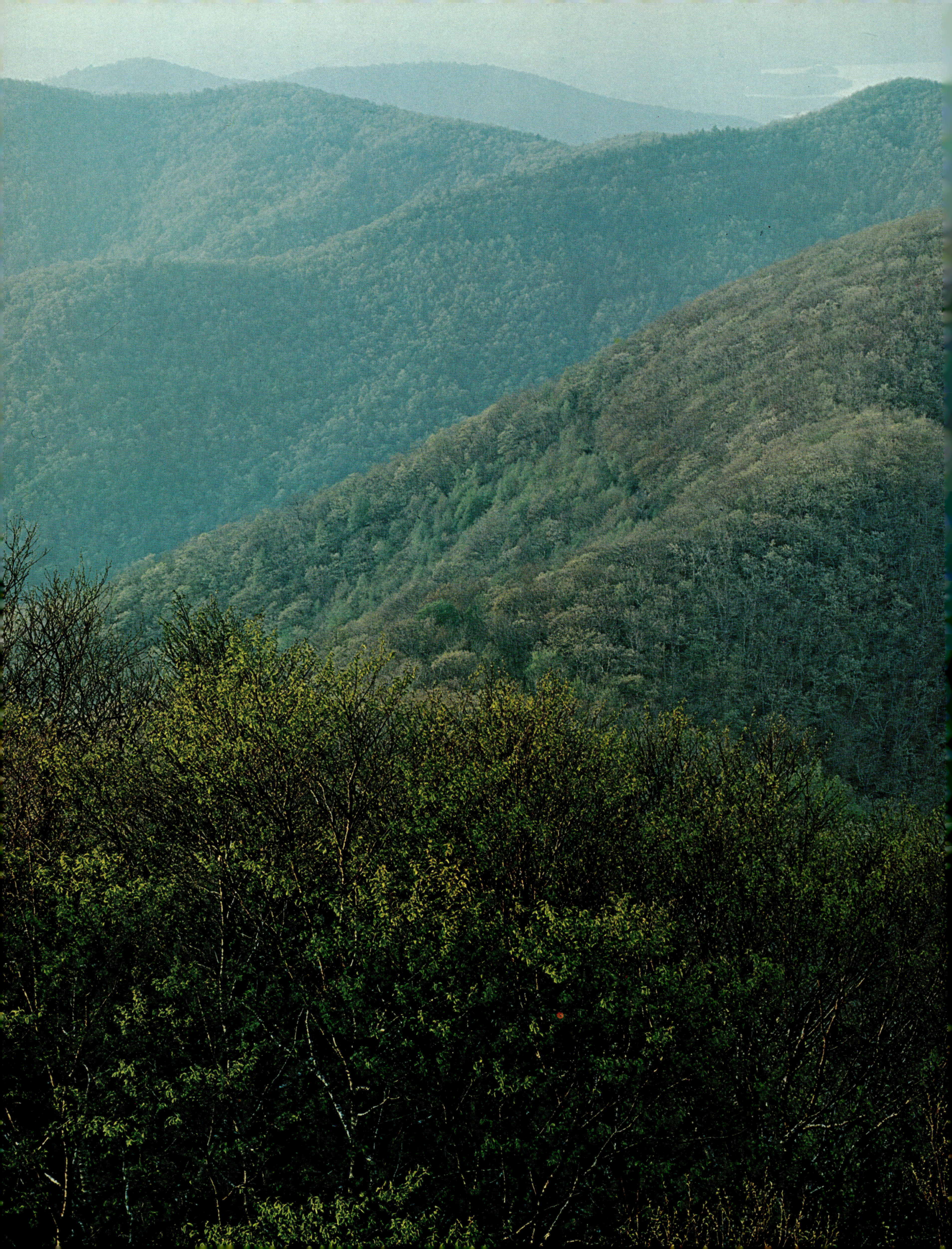

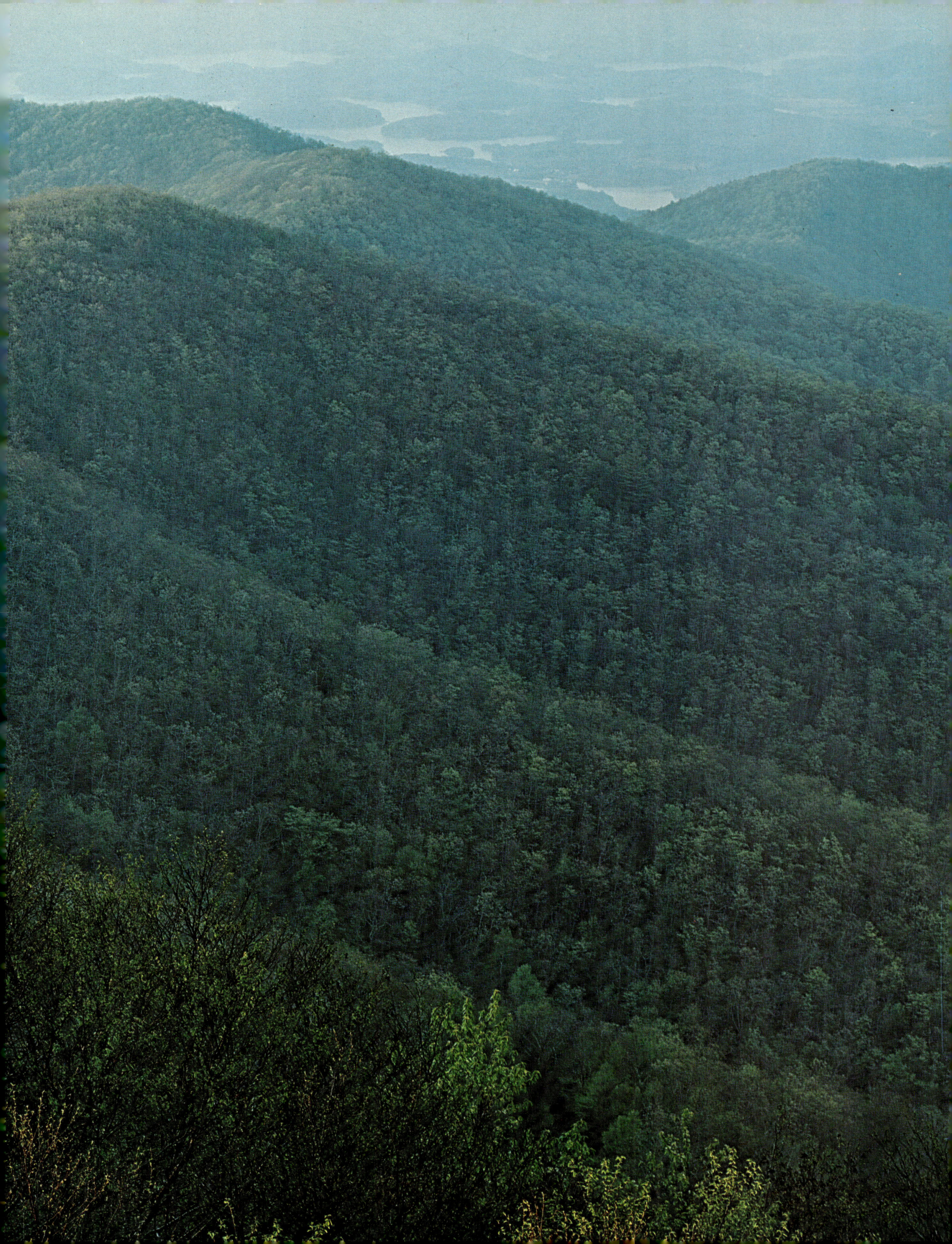

After a six-mile hike in deep snow and a fall
into icy east fork of the Chattooga River,
photographer encountered "Ellicott's Rock"
approximately 100 feet downstream.
Ellicott and some mules established the famous
"Rock" that marks the corner of North Carolina,
South Carolina and Georgia.

This now timid and dammed river once roared and thrashed its way down the treacherous Tallulah Gorge. The Cherokees bestowed upon the river a name that reflected its original character—Tallulah, meaning Terrible.
Pages 44 and 45: Betty's Creek, where leaves catch each drop of the magic light; Dillard.

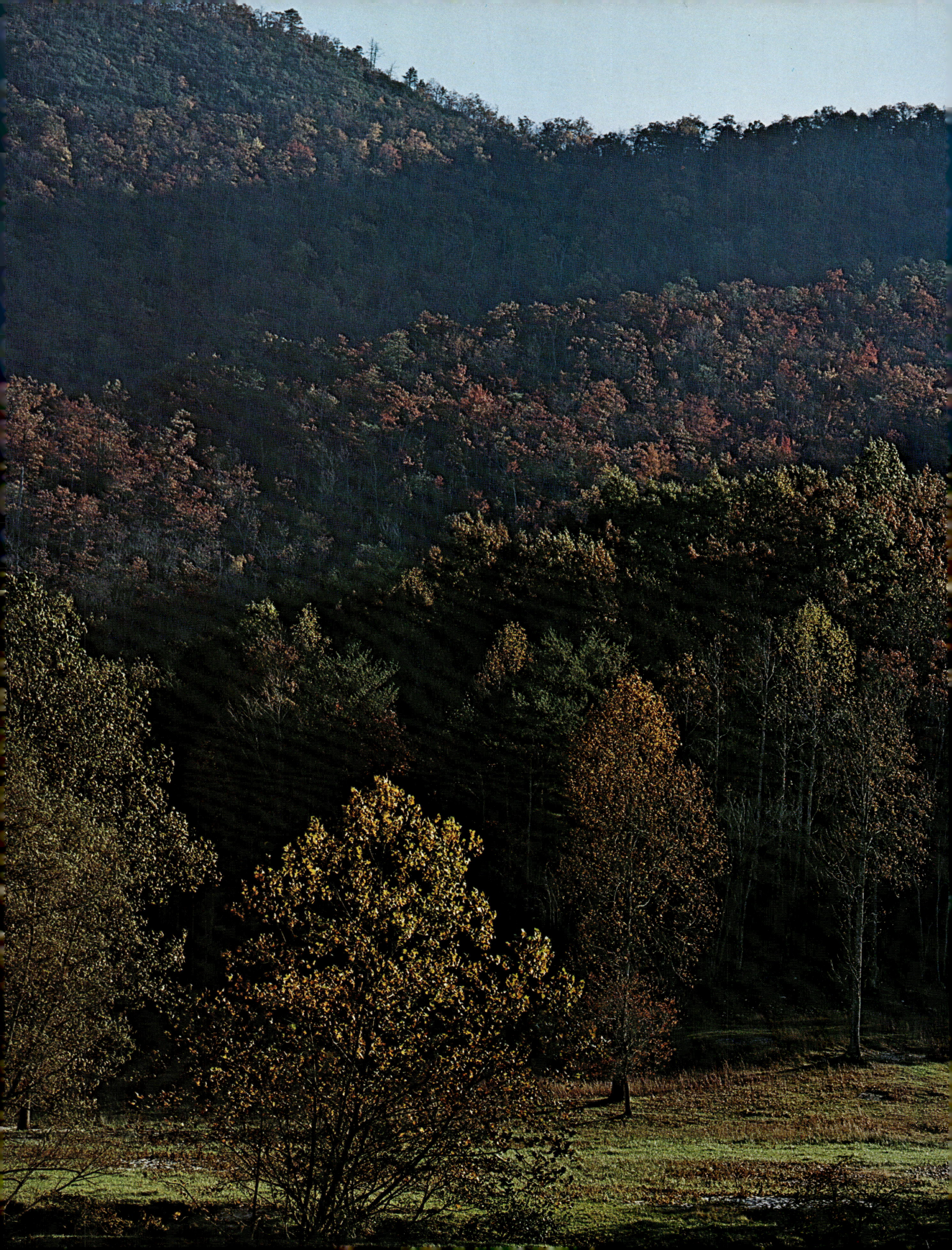

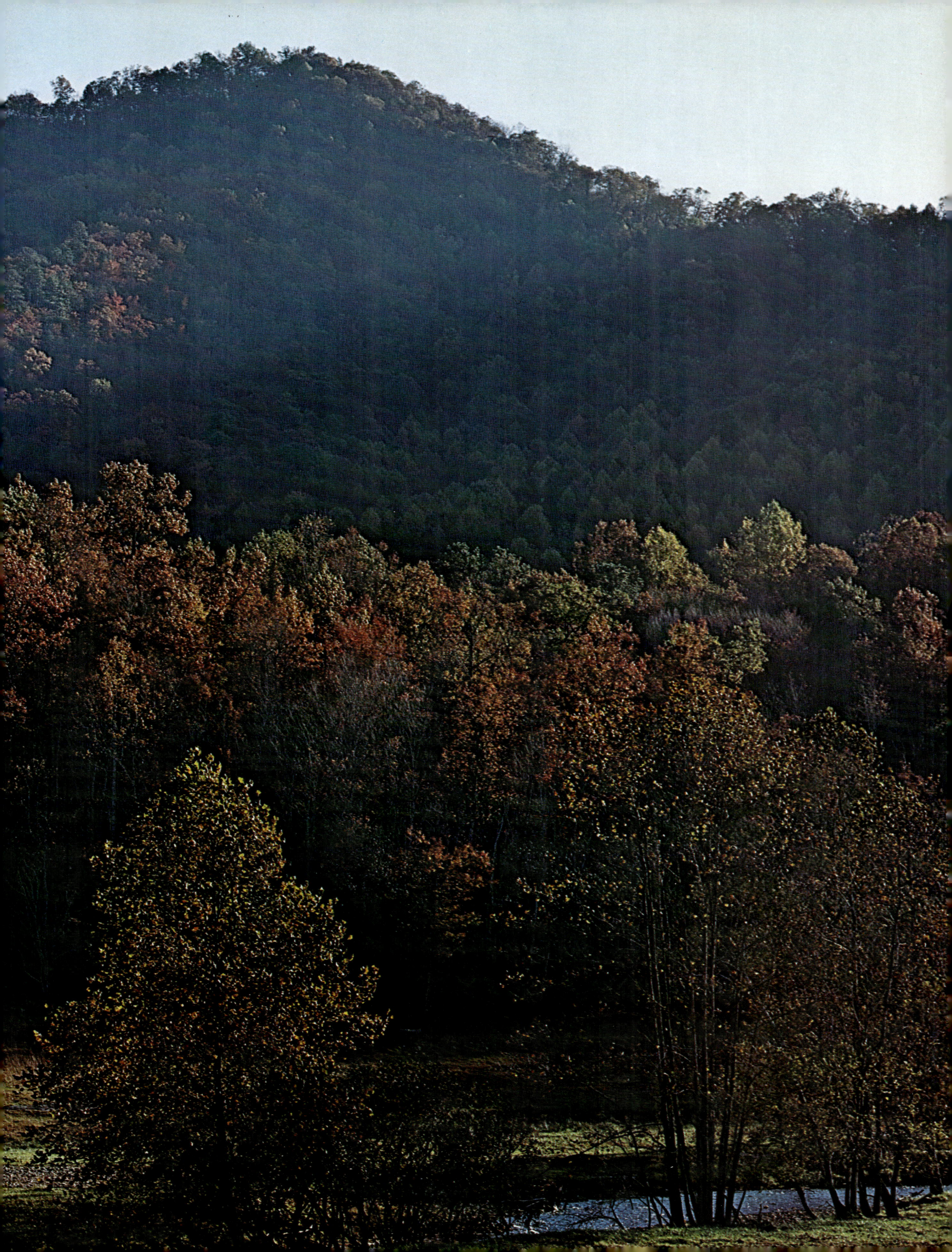

An expanse of exploding light rays and ancient
cloud mariners travel in a westward direction
from Brasstown Bald.

A celebration of maple color breathes against
the long-leaf pines in Tallulah Gorge.

Beneath the spreading maples, the swift west fork of the wild and scenic Chattooga River, rushes into an unknown future in Three Forks Wilderness. Right: The pure water on Pigeon Mountain is filtered thousands of times as it makes its way through limestone caverns. "The Pocket", Lafayette.

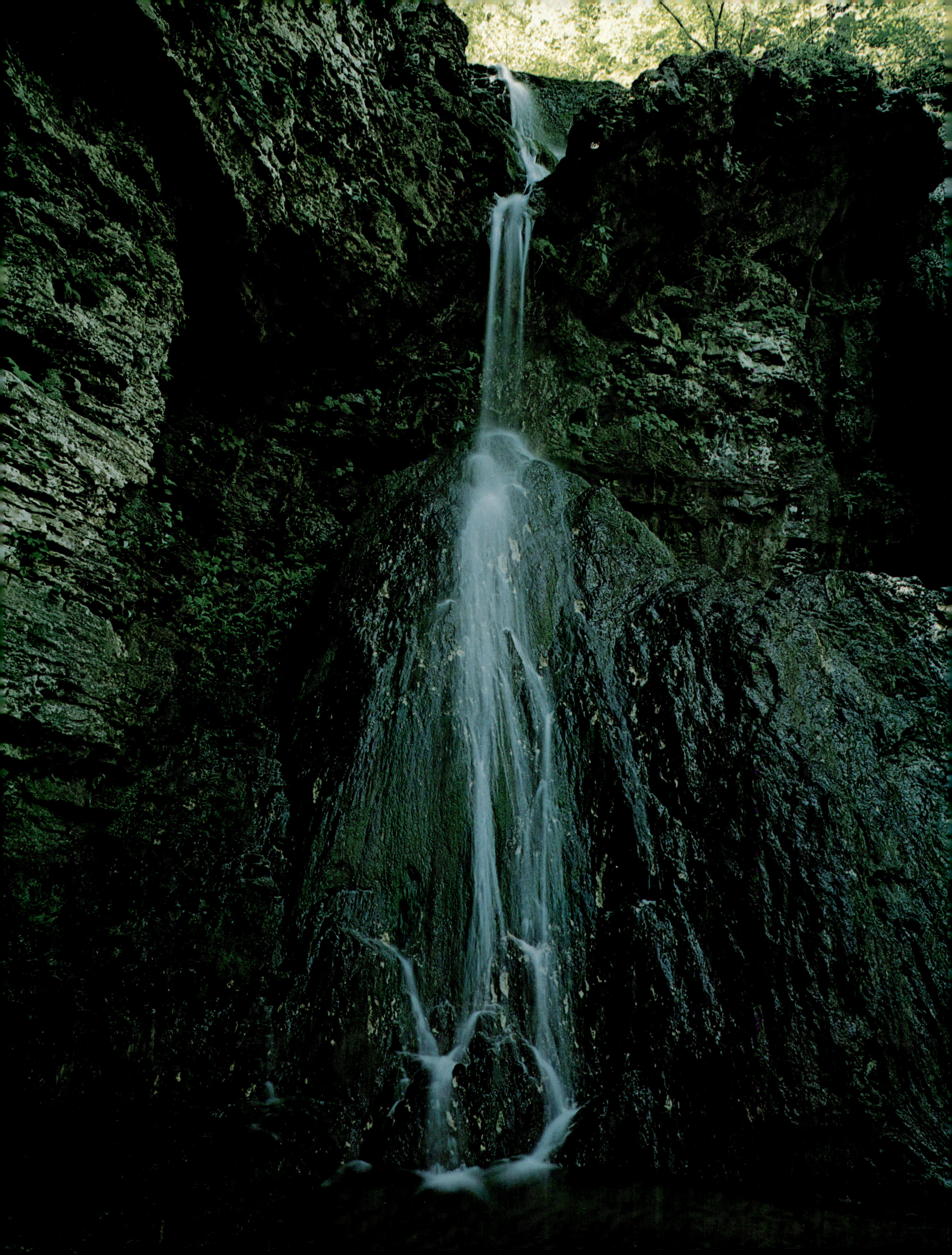

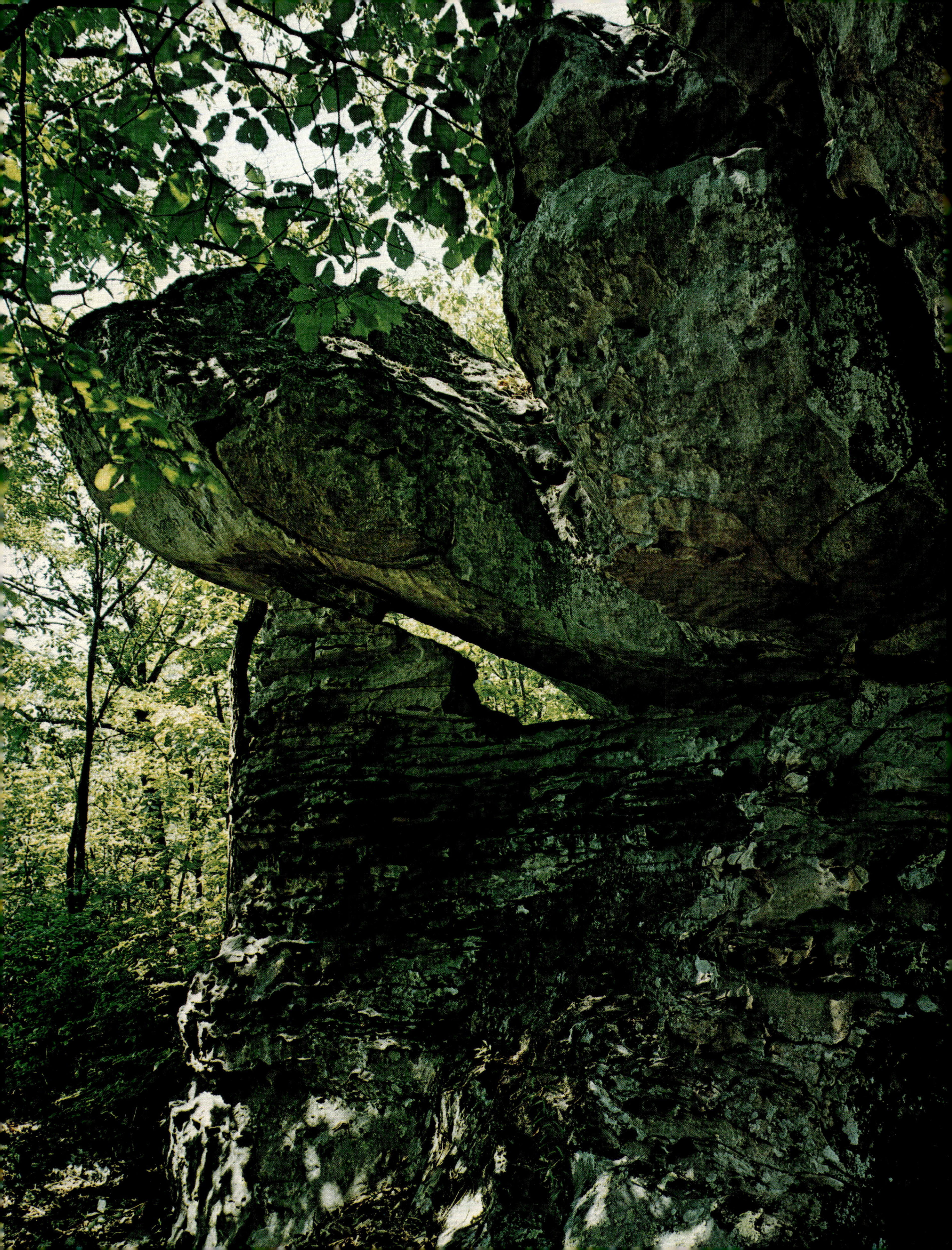

Early morning expansion of energy over Rabun Gap. Left: Monolithic protrusions in the wilderness, Rock Town, Pigeon Mountain.

This beastly rock spirit clings to an obscure
cliff in the middle of Rock Town,
Pigeon Mountain.

Roadside bonanza of exuberant fall color surrounds U.S. Highway Number 76 west of Clayton. Turkey Gap, Chattahooche National Forest.

Could this be a sacred ceremonial center where eroded workings of nature were modified by ancient cultures to accentuate natural shapes and create deities, creatures and animal spirits? This enigma contains giant 30 foot pot, a turtle image and a large griffin-type image, Rock Town, Pigeon Mountain.

Cherokee legend reveals their predecessors as blue-eyed, fair-skinned bearded people. They named them "Moon-Eyed People" because of nocturnal vision. Maybe this monolith bares a sealed past in Rock Town, Pigeon Mountain. Pages 56 and 57: Camera captures unusual sun streak, Rising Fawn, Lookout Mountain.

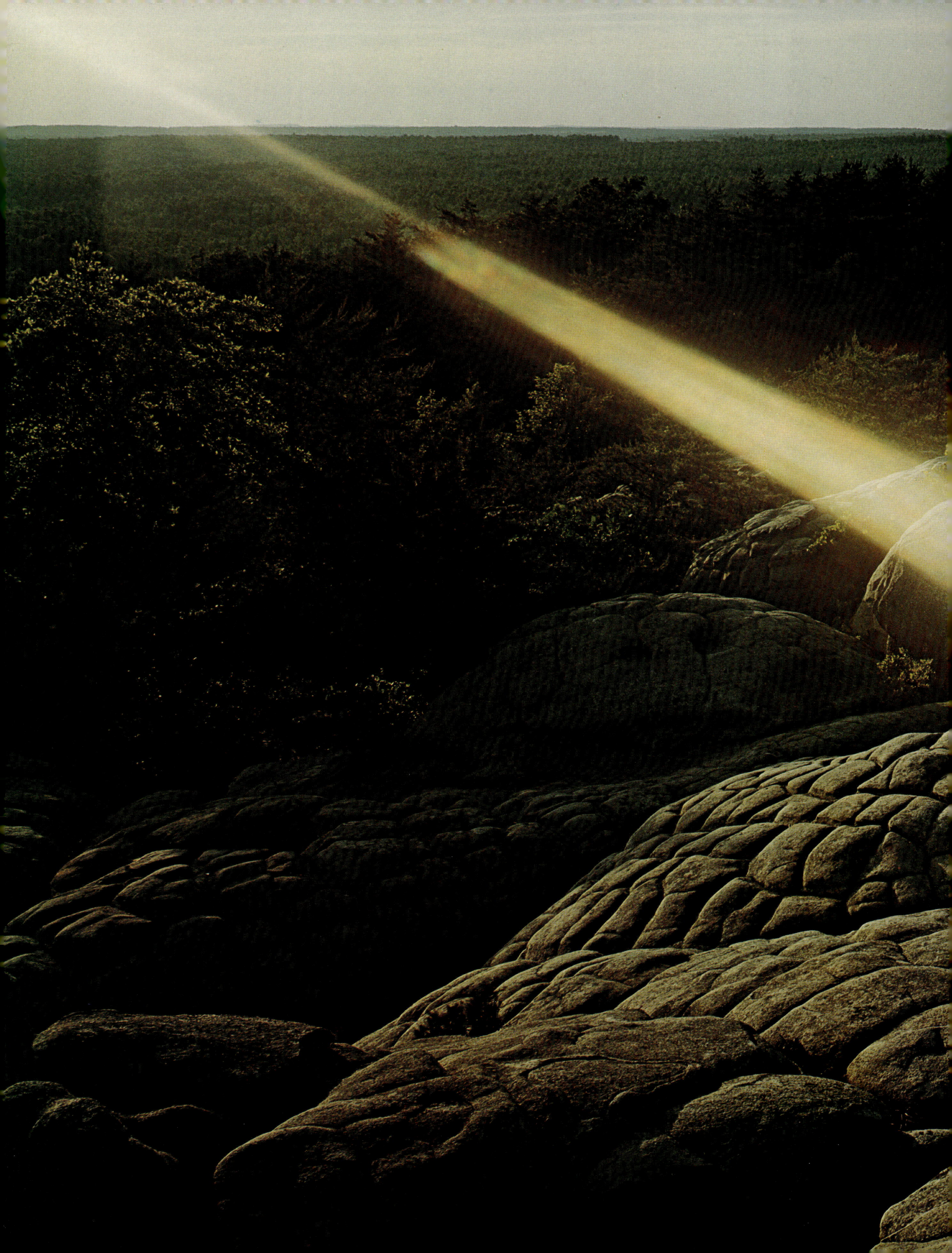

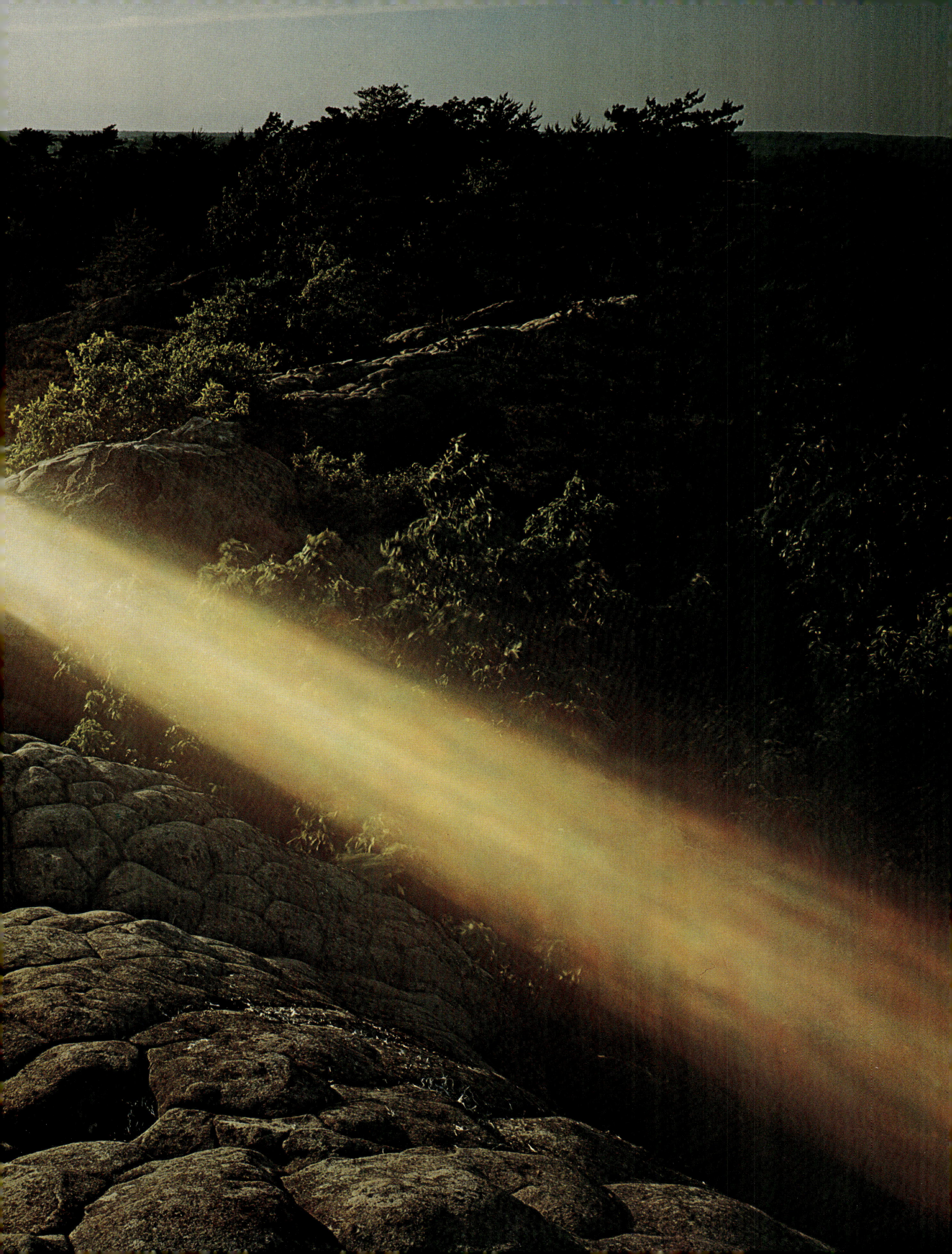

Time has molded this limestone into a stone mosaic painting near Rock Town, Pigeon Mountain.

At base of Blue Hole Falls presides a one-eyed creature whose hair is very electric, Swallow Creek Wildlife Management Area. Pages 60 and 61: Jack's River Falls in the Cohutta Mountains, a major contributor to the largest wilderness area in the state. Cohutta Wilderness, Chattahoochee National Forest.

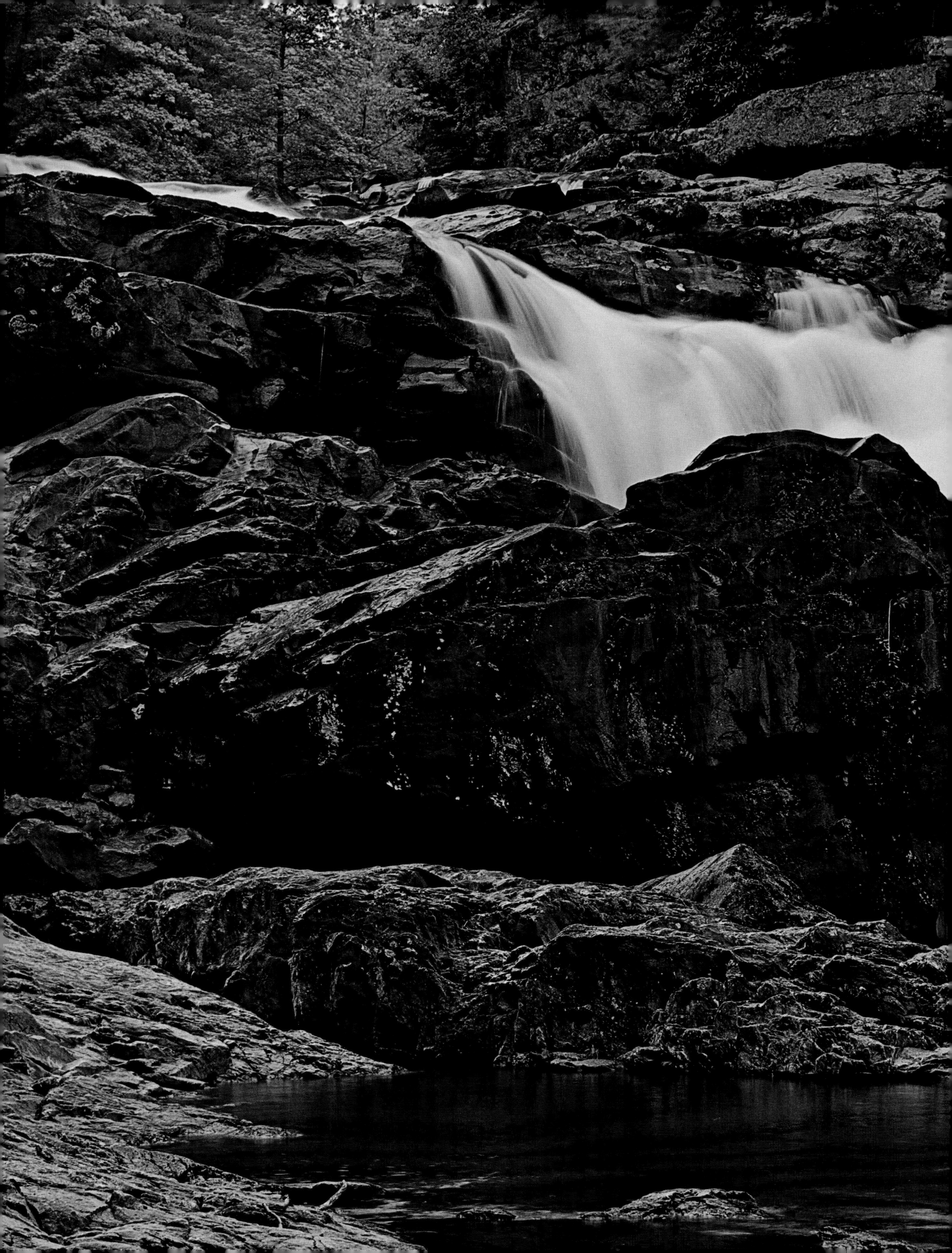

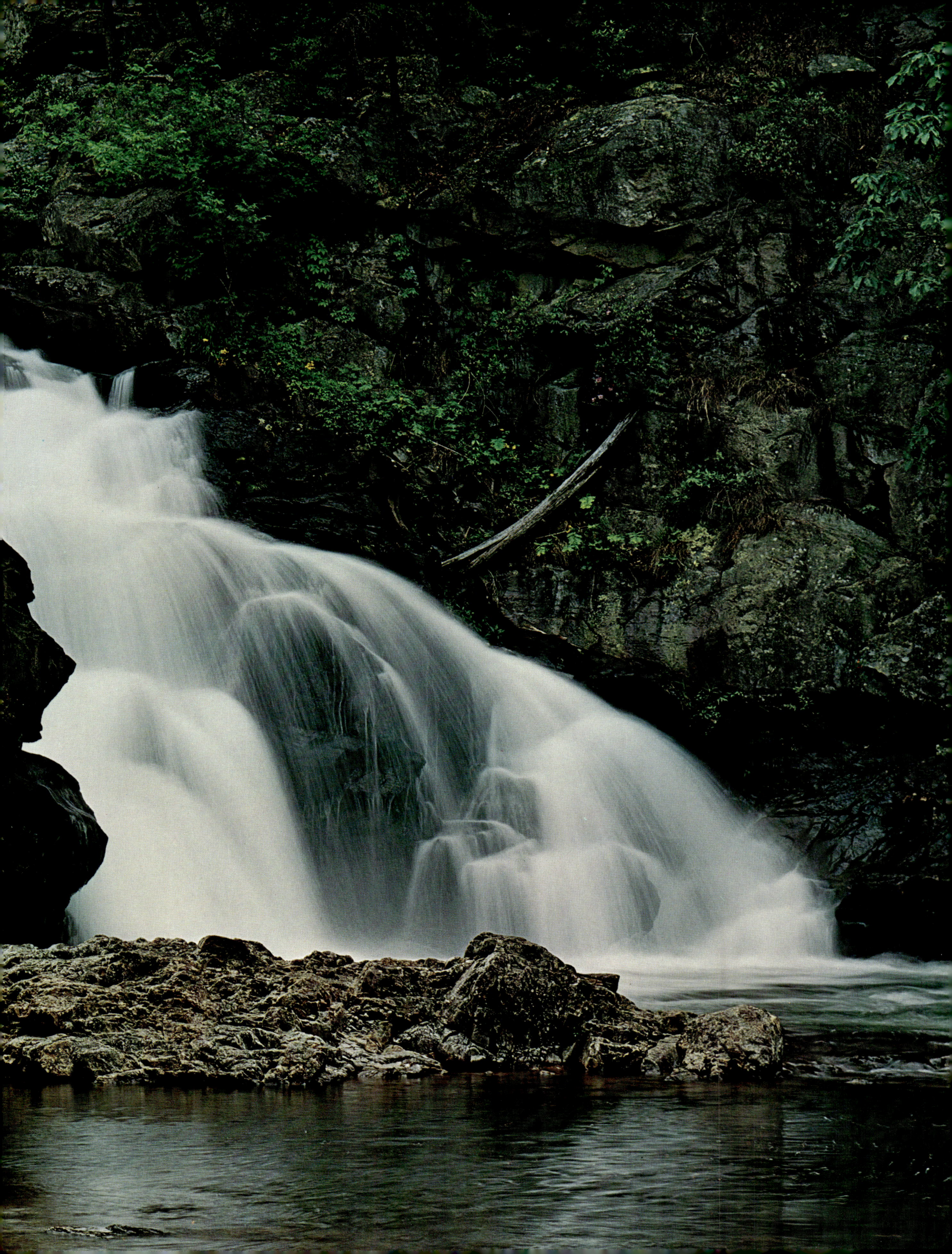

An endless supply of mother earth's milk seemingly pours down the golden cliffs of Toccoa Falls; Toccoa.

Valleys surrounding distant Mt. Yonah were named for the Indian lovers, Sautee and Nacoochee. View from the Richard Russell Scenic Highway.

Two early spring trilliums join in their own
perfect circle, found in Amicalola
State Park.

The immense Chattooga River challenges a dwarfed kayaker as he runs Section Four considered the most spectacular white water in the state.

Pure water possesses the secret to life along the west fork of the raging, scenic Chattooga River in the Three Forks Wilderness.

Long Creek Falls, a swift tributary of surging water, joins Section Four of the Chattooga River.

Late evening fog pulsates out of an Appalachian canyon near Helen.

Nostalgic spirit of a primeval river slowly weaves its way into the early years of men. Section Four of the wild and rushing Chattooga River.

A pigeon flock glides softly into a cloud shadow
playground. View from Blue Ridge Dam.

The first signs of spring unwrap themselves along Holcomb Creek in Three Forks Wilderness. Pages 72 and 73: Deep in the heart of the Cohutta Mountains a hardwood cove forest ascends over a herb ground cover. Image on Hickory Ridge, State Highway Number 2, Cohutta Wilderness.

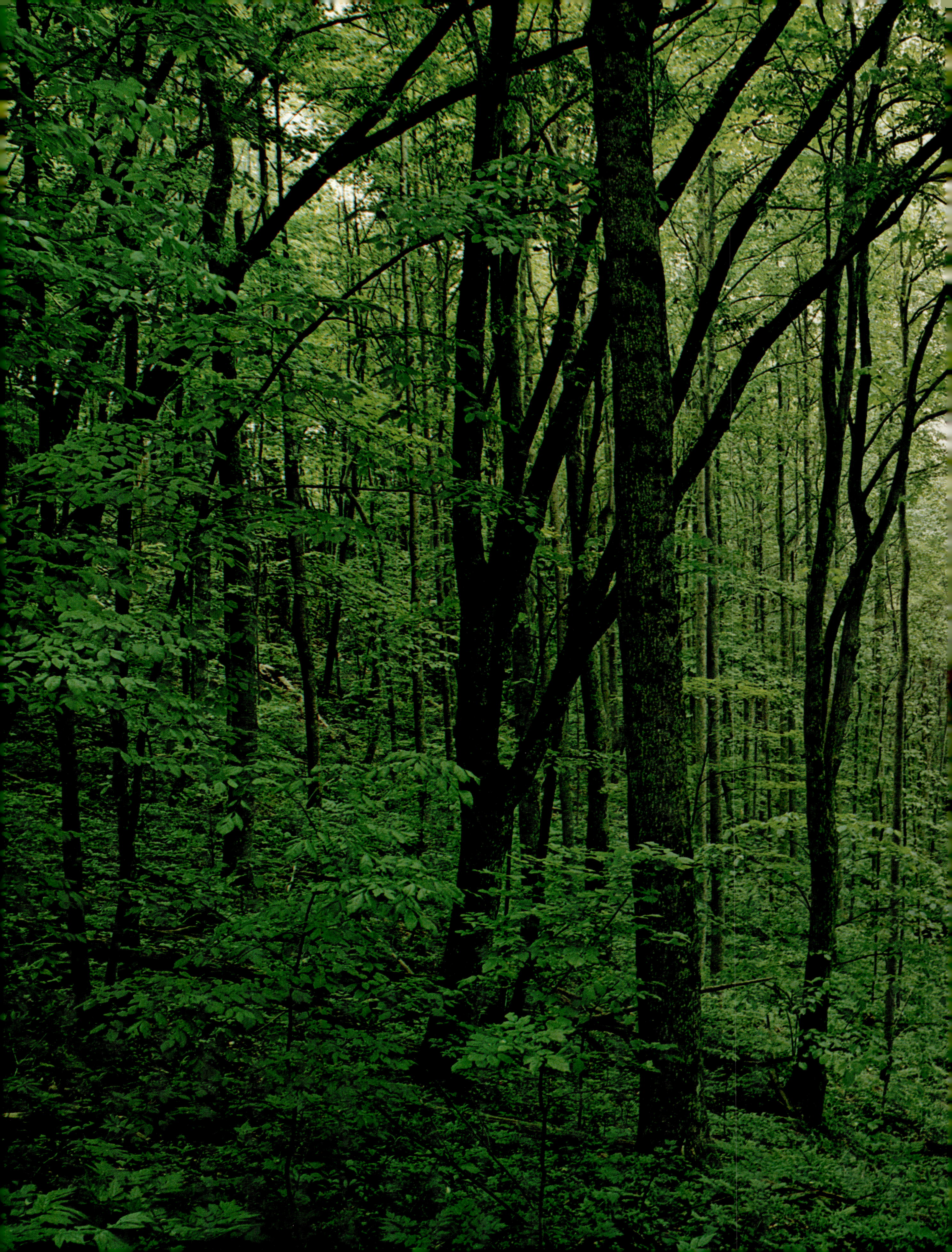

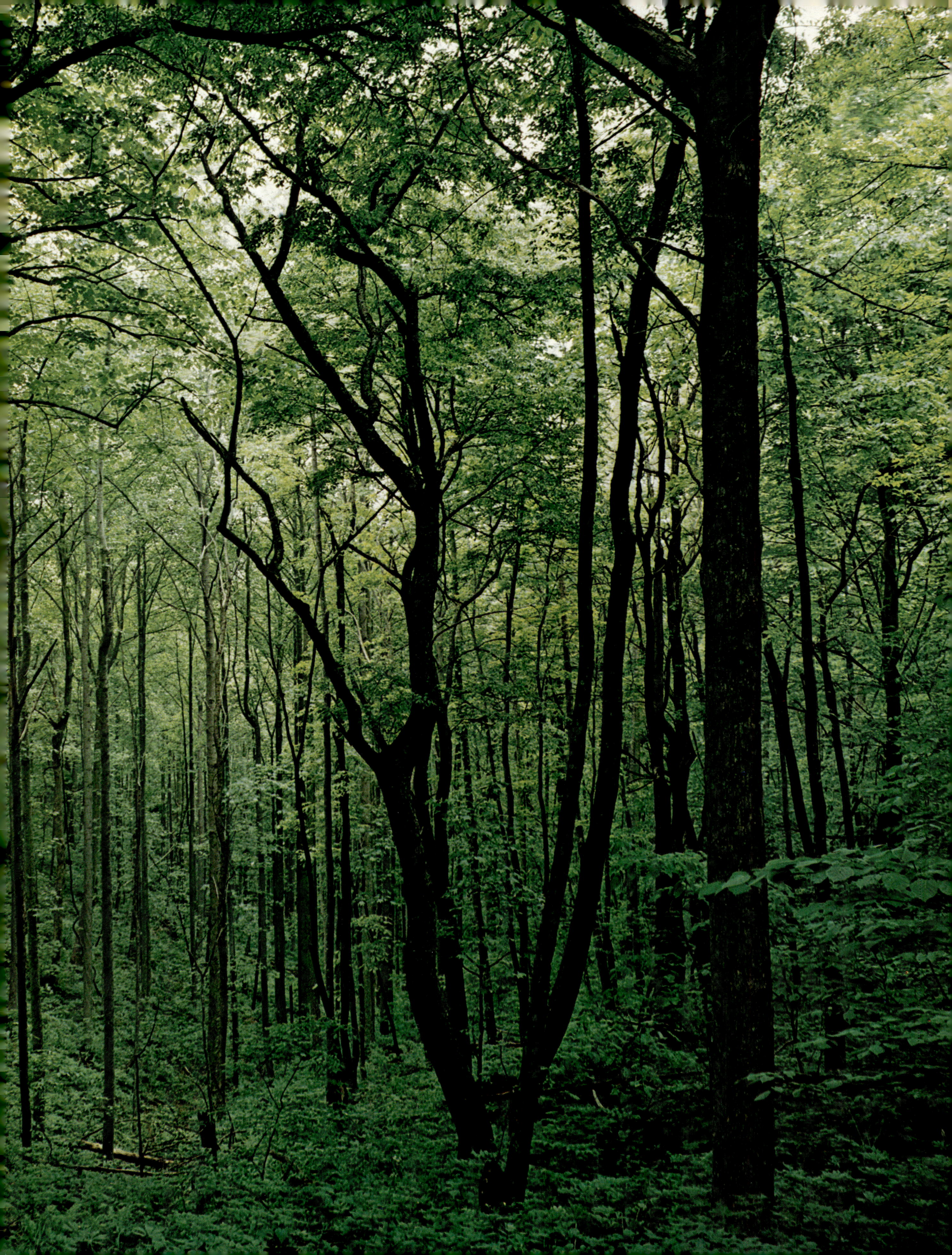

The crystal-clear Anna Ruby Falls at Unicoi State Park seems to come sparkling out of the summer tree tops, near Helen.

A field of buttercups dances wildly in a mild summer breeze, in vicinity of Ellijay. Pages 76 and 77: From the highest point on Lookout Mountain is seen McLemore Cove and the distant Pigeon Mountain.

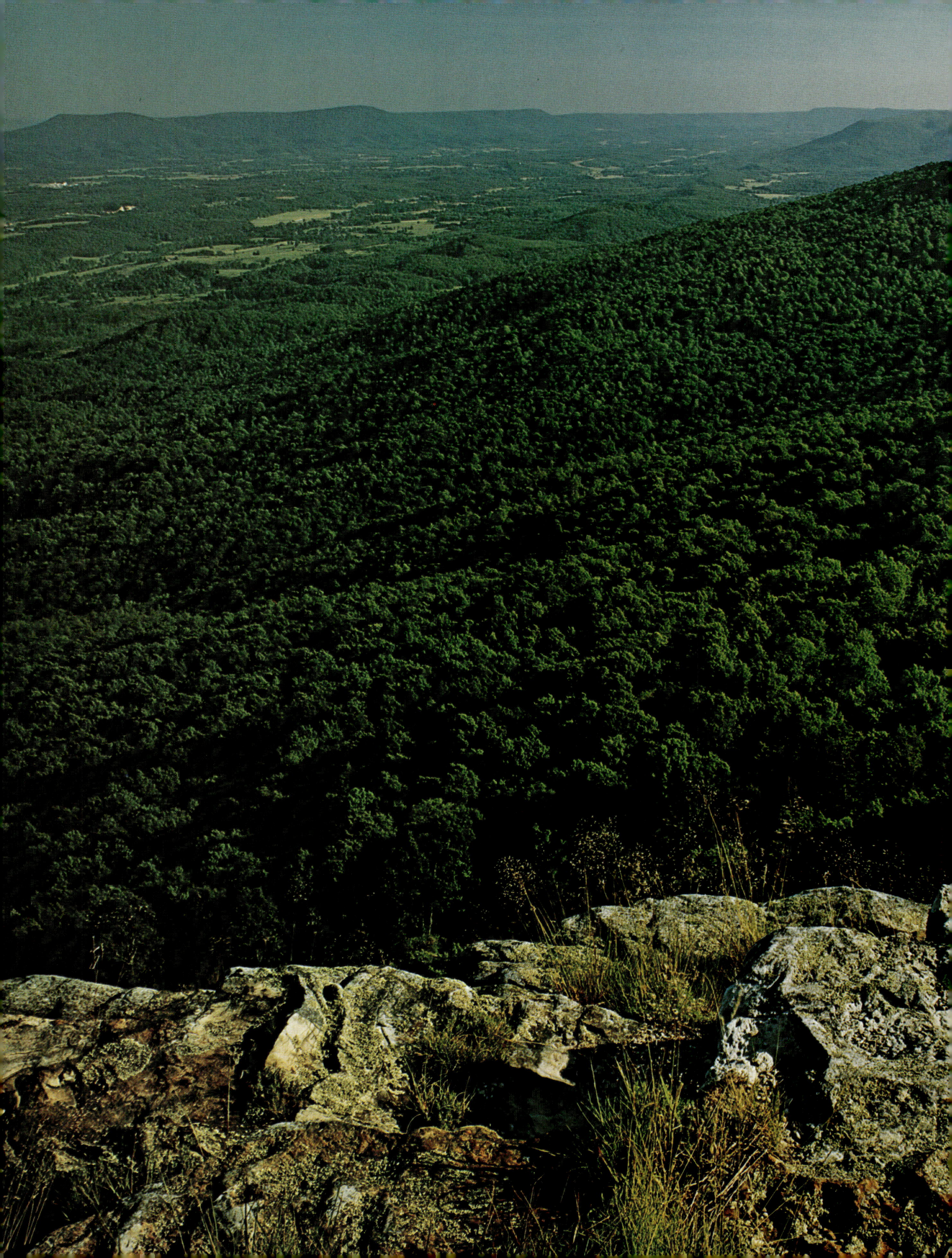

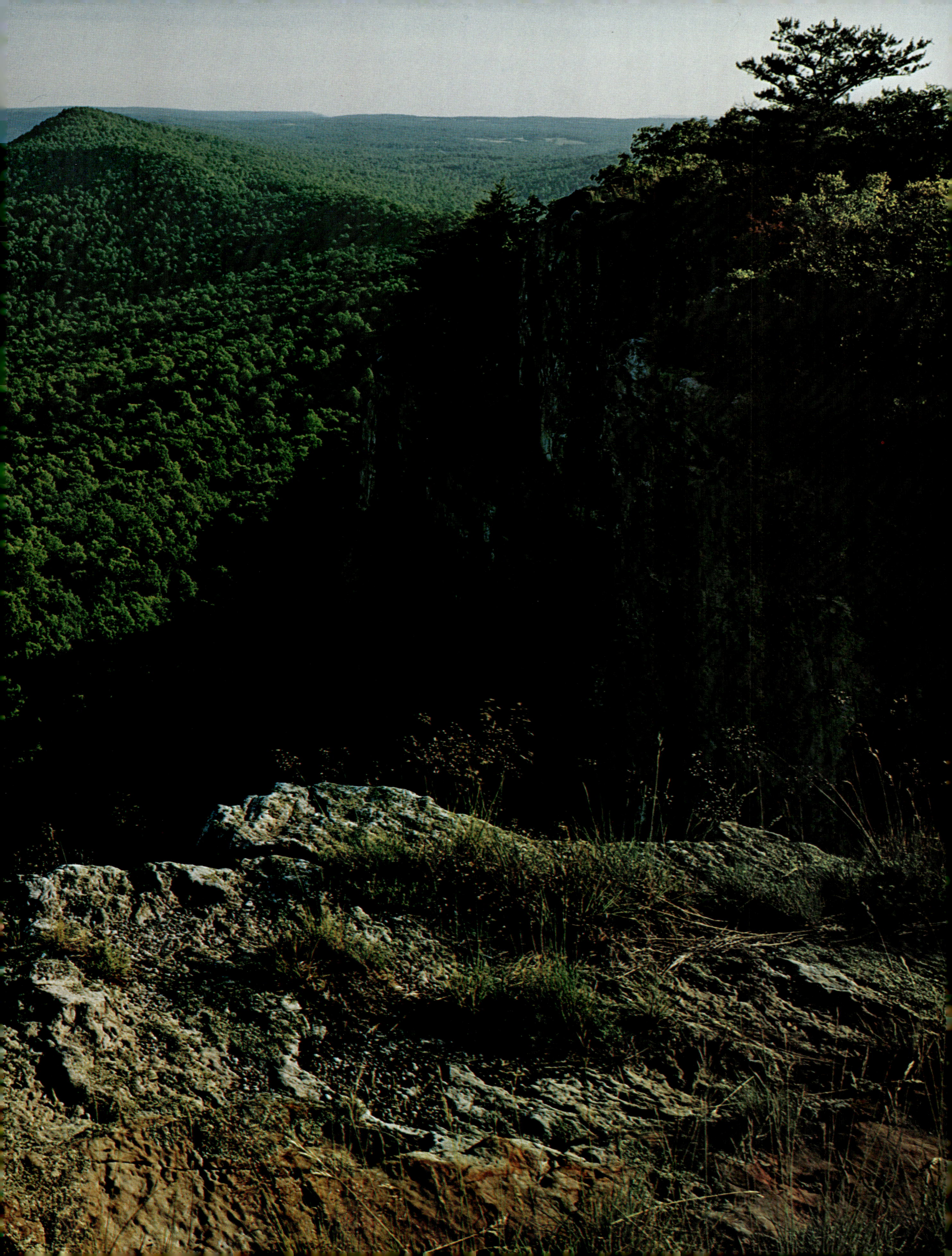

Ethereal cloud vagabonds hover over a field
of buttercups, outside Ellijay.

A lush summer vale of rhododendrons and birch cover the cool spring-fed waters of the upper Tallulah River. Coleman River Wildlife Management area, Clayton.

This fall drops several hundred feet to form a beautiful pool in the Amicalola Falls State Park. View looking toward Burnt and Oglethorpe Mountains. Right: On moist fern-laden slopes of the Cohutta Mountains black birch have stood guard for centuries. Potato Patch Mountain, Cohutta Wildlife Management area, Blue Ridge.

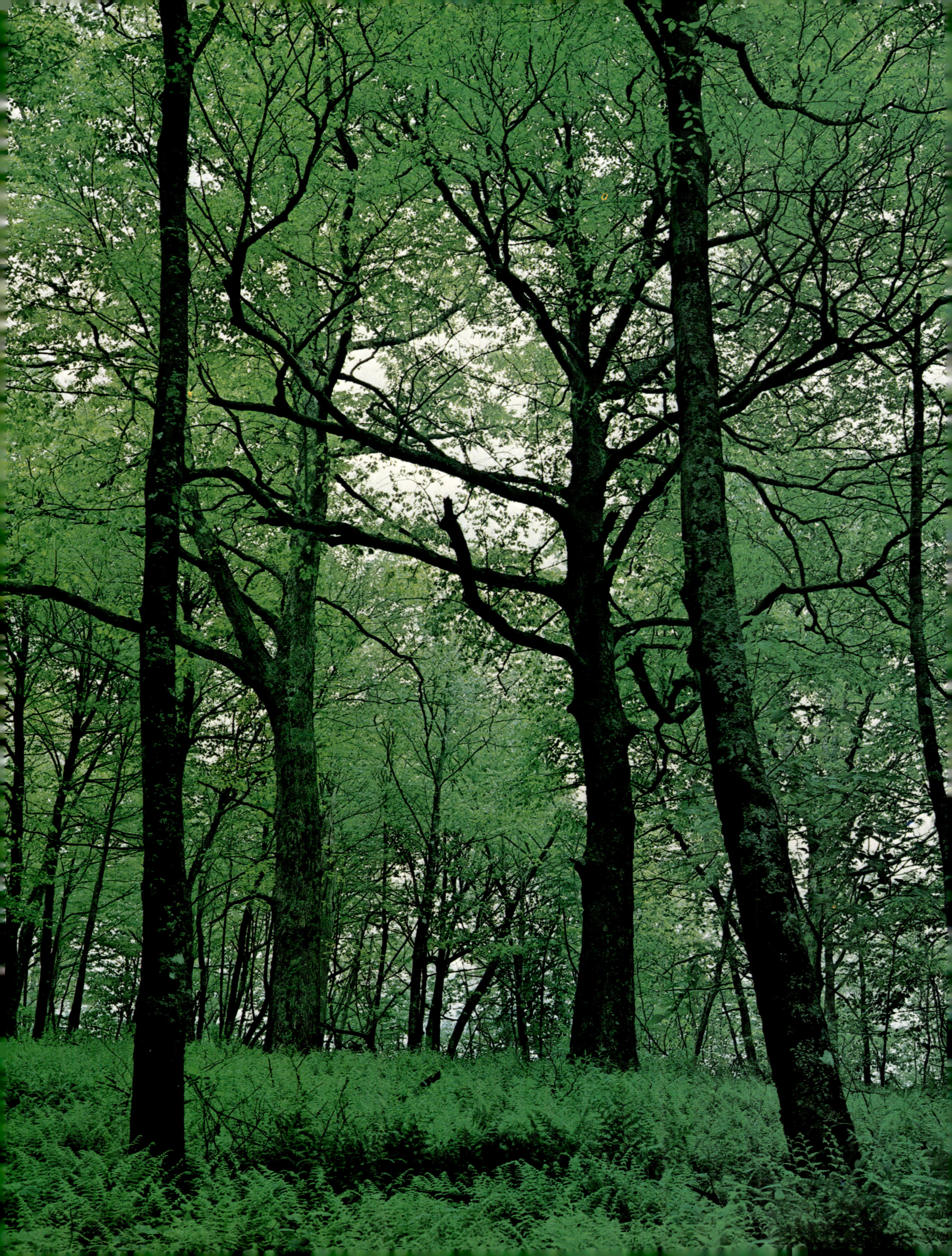

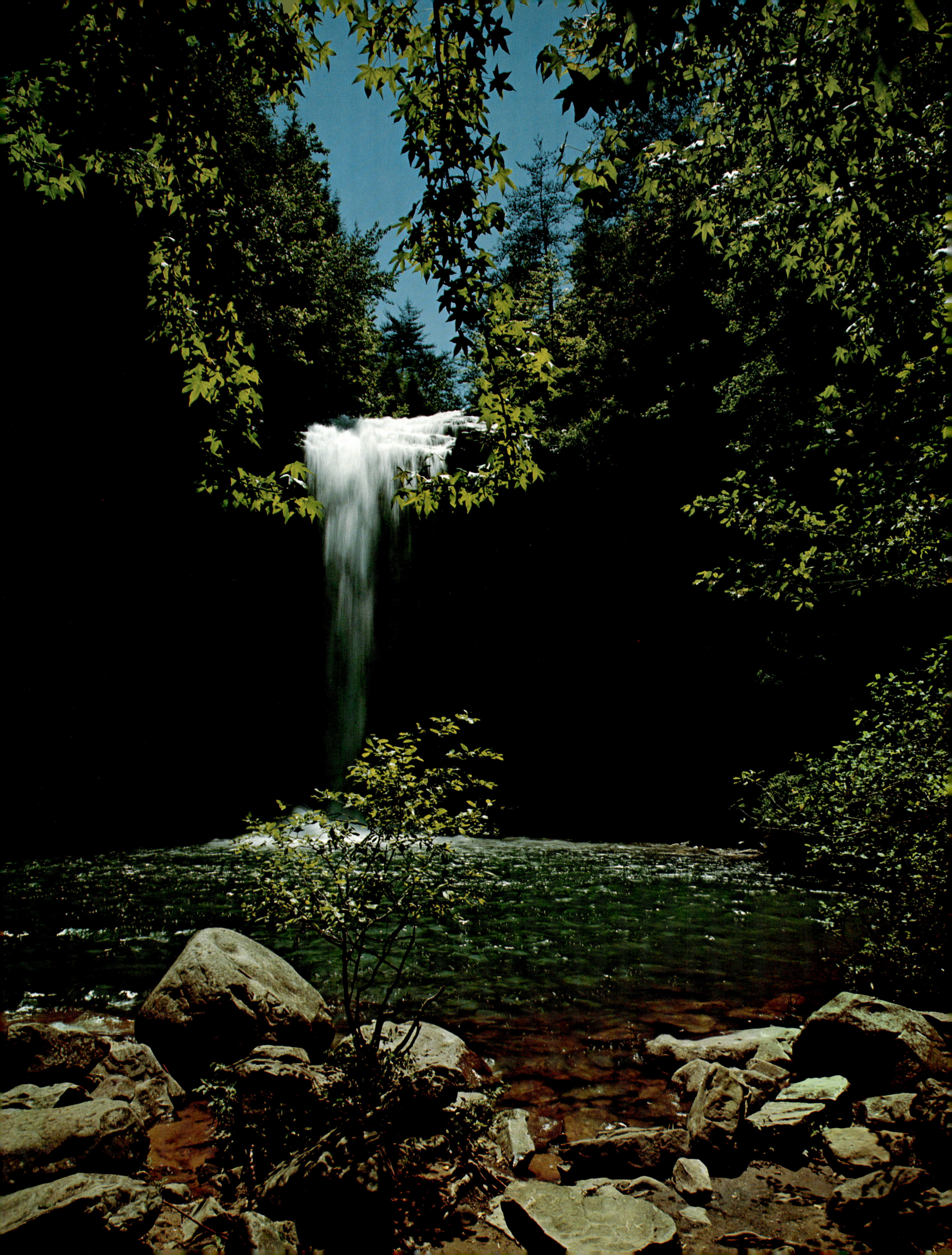

The head waters of Coopers Creek flow through one of Georgia's unique scenic areas. Blue Ridge, Chattahoochee National Forest.
Left: The emerald green waters of the upper falls on Daniel Creek cascade down Cloudland Canyon State Park, Rising Fawn.

In this hardwood pocket of green,
the dogwood seeks its place in the spring sun,
south of Gaddistown.

The forested mesas of West Georgia give birth
to a lush summer canyon. Cloudland Canyon
State Park, Rising Fawn, near the
Alabama border.

The north rim of Cloudland Canyon shimmers
under the morning light of a crisp fall day.
Cloudland Canyon State Park, Rising Fawn.

Late evening illumination skims down the slopes of Lookout Mountain. Pigeon Mountain, a flat mesa, looms across the placid valley. Pages 88 and 89: The immense cliffs of Cloudland in Cloudland Canyon State Park.

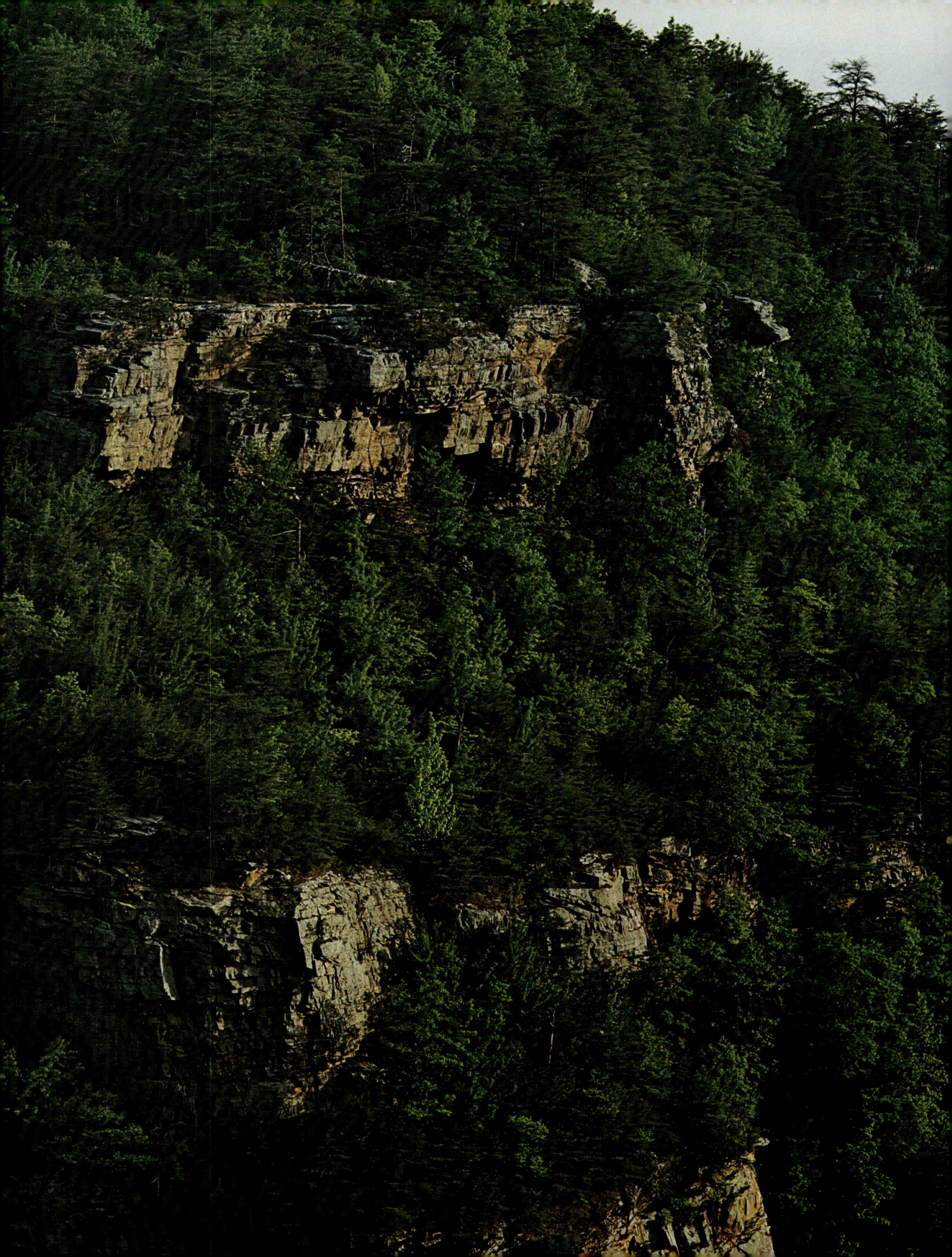

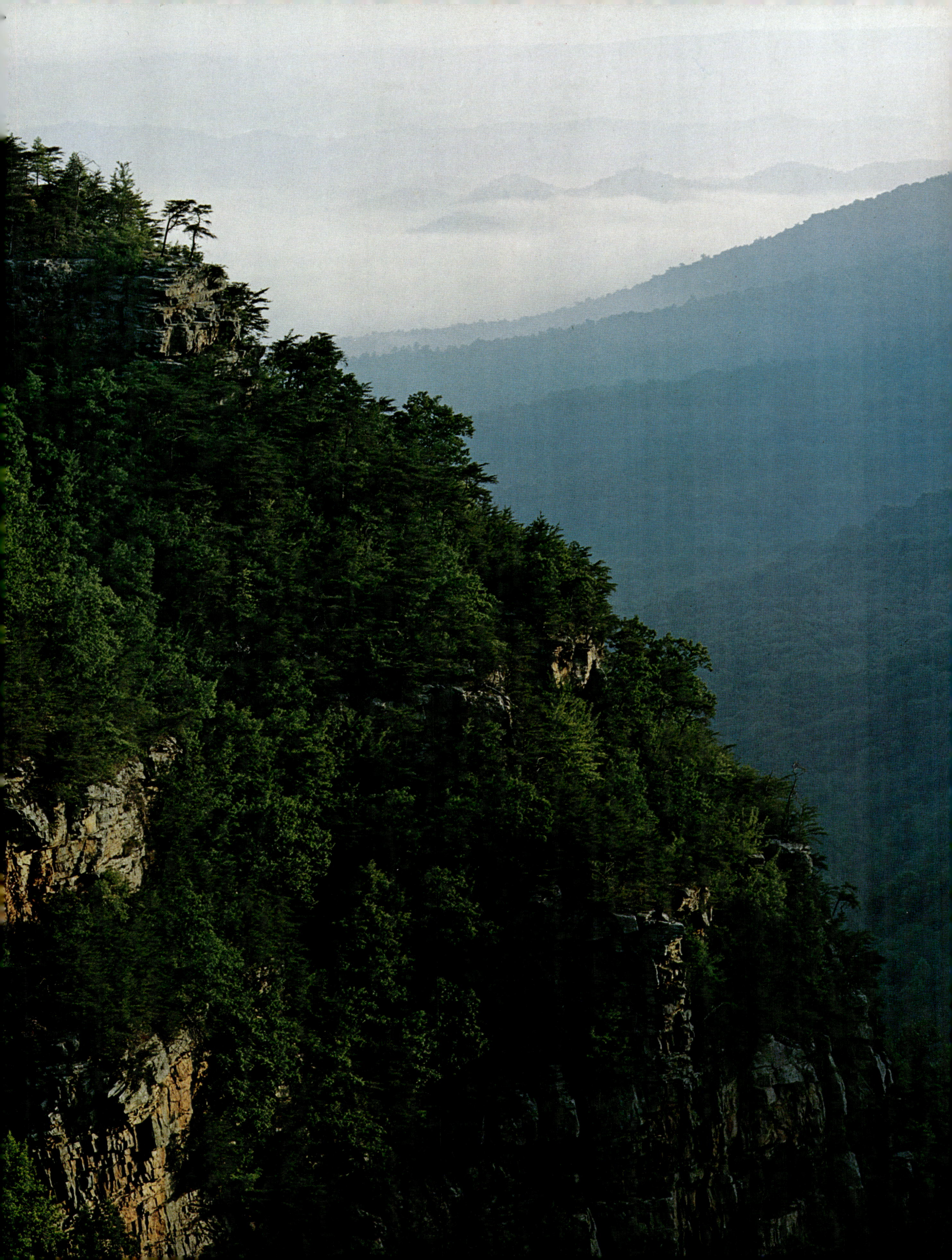

A luscious spread of azaleas and dogwood
intimately decorate the piney woods,
Callaway Gardens, Pine Mountain.

Beyond this glorious tulip poplar, the escarpment edge of a Gainesville Ridge descends into the distant Piedmont; Cornelia. Pages 92 and 93: A rosy sunset rests over metropolitan Atlanta. Vista from the top of Stone Mountain.

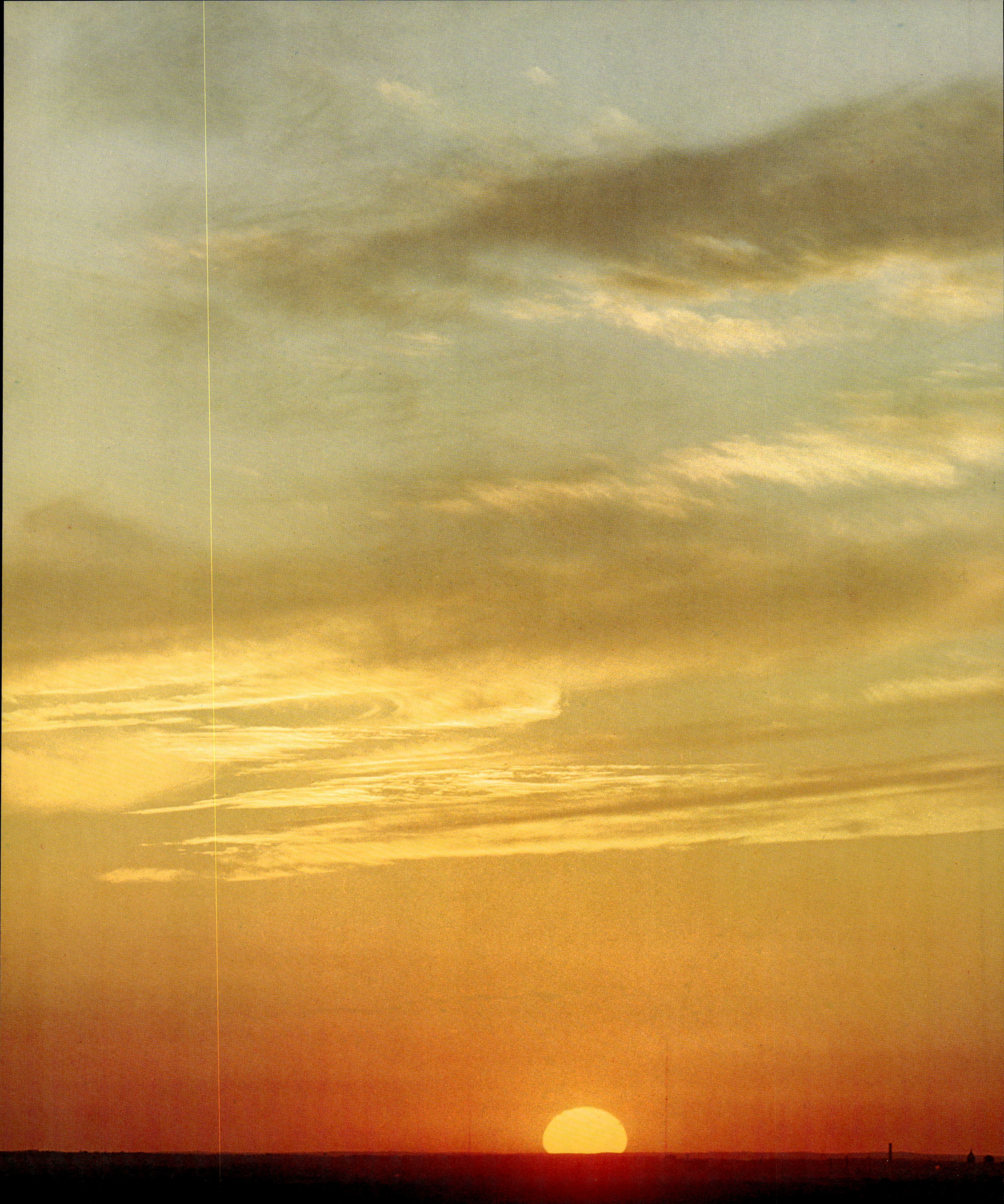

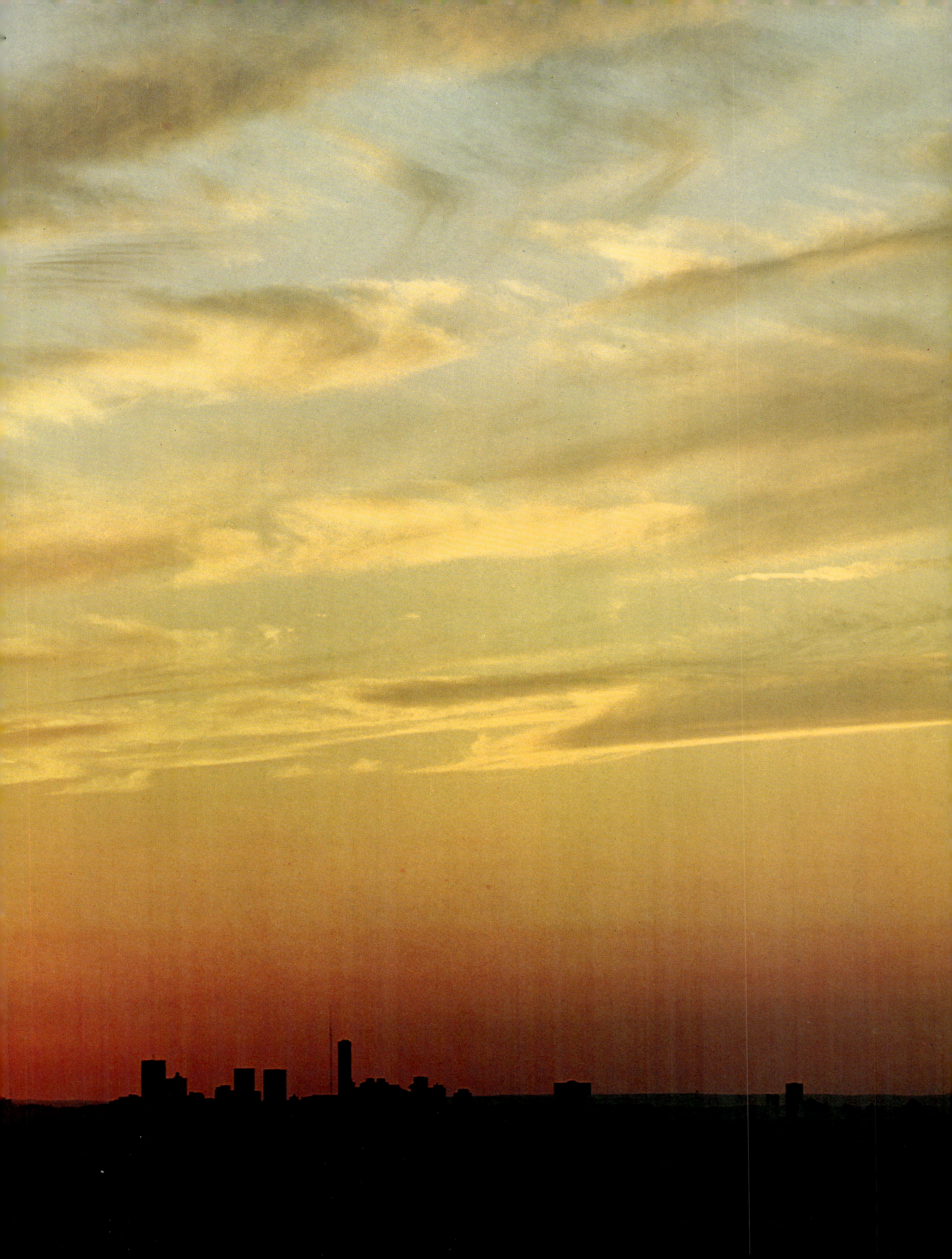

The largest single piece of exposed granite in the world abruptly emerges before a full Piedmont moon in Stone Mountain Memorial Park.

The torch-bearing lady of freedom presides
over the golden-crested State Capitol in Atlanta.

Sunbeams flicker over Alcovy Shoals Falls,
near the community of Covington.

A mellow spring brook meanders through
Pleasant Valley, near the edge of Gaddistown.

In early March the shallow soil-filled dish
gardens of Panola Mountain State Park become
overflowing with a miniature pinkish-red glow.
It is created by a rare plant called
"Diamorpha cymosa".

A very soft mossy gray rock provides a hiding place for rare plants of Panola Mountain State Park.

Within Panola Mountain State Park is a
fully-protected granite outcrop where scientific
research is made on rare plant communities.
It is one of the few examples in the world where
soil formation can be observed in a
natural laboratory.

The wild Chattahoochee River still exists within the boundaries of Atlanta. The Chattahoochee River Park cliffs expose a mixture of pines, oaks and hickories.

A dramatic cloud racing past Pine Mountain
colors the earth with an evening burst
of magical light.

This three-week-old owlet looks rather perplexed to find himself in a sea of daffodils, Callaway Gardens, Pine Mountain. Pages 104 and 105: Near the central region of the state spring rains bring a flood of water into High Falls State Park.

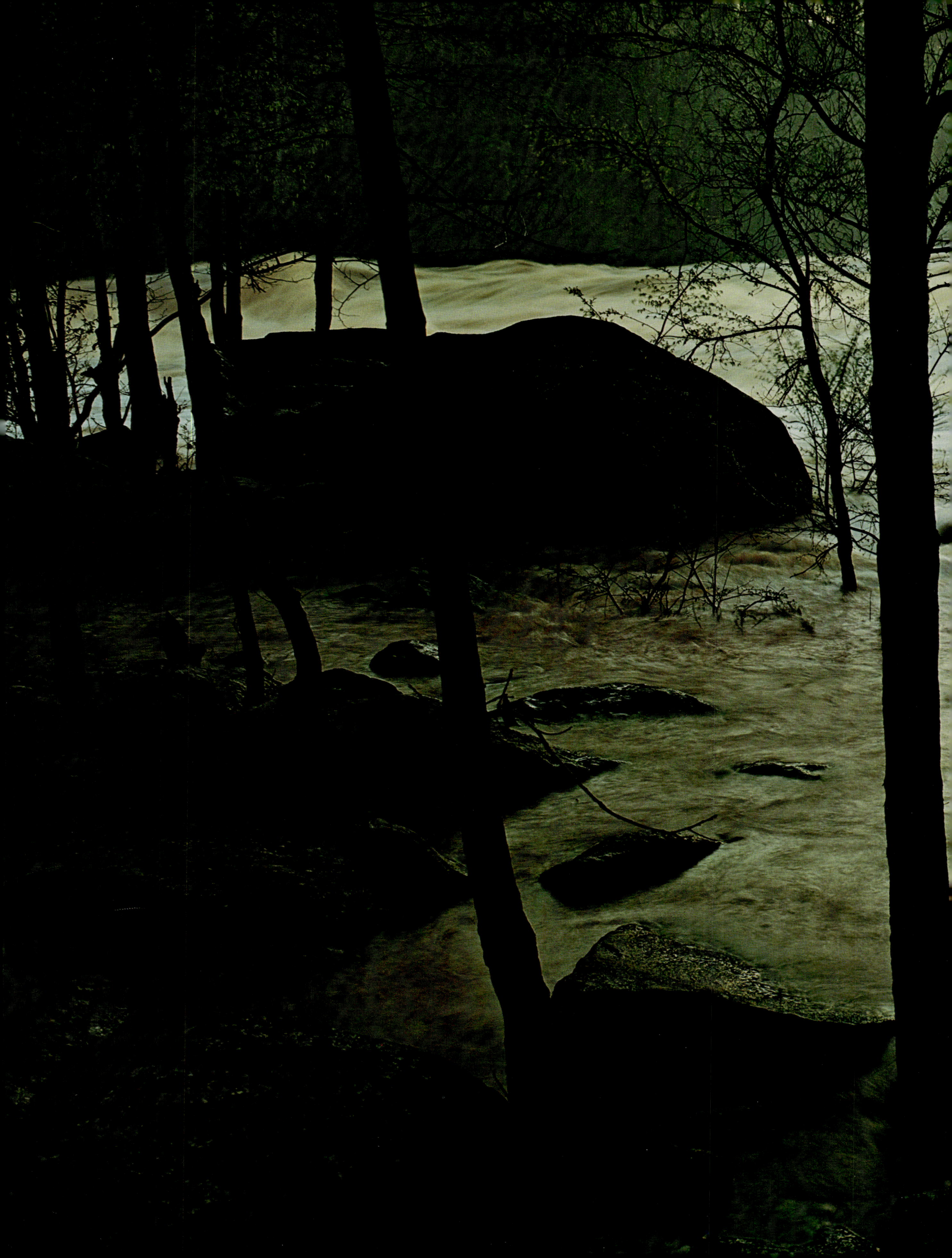

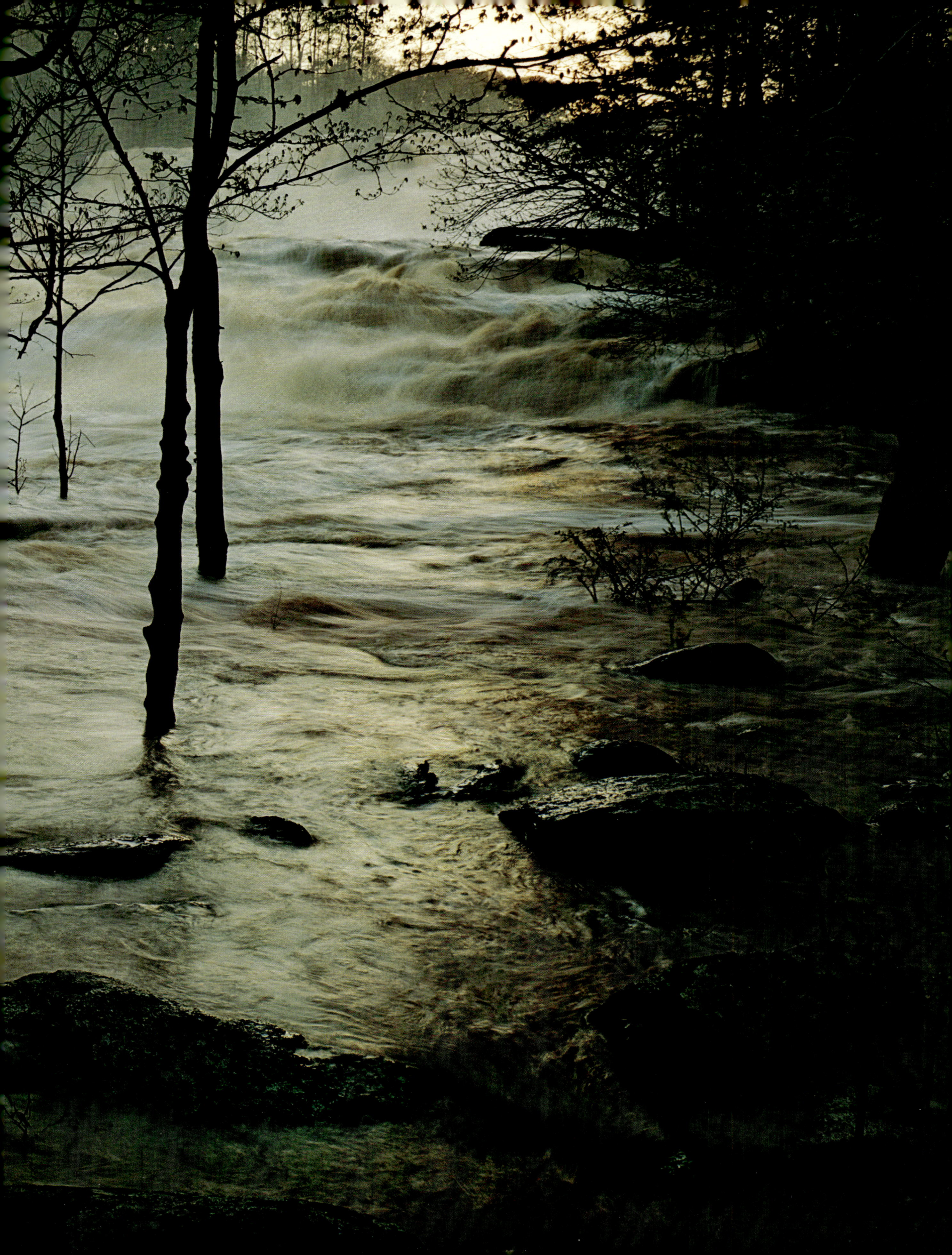

Elevated view of the Chattahoochee River displays an exposed river bottom during an especially dry autumn. Chattahoochee River Park, Atlanta.

The crisp ozone-filled air swirls past a Piedmont forest beyond Cornelia. Pages 108 and 109: Southeast of Atlanta are mesa-type mountains of granite, capped with quartzite rock. This billion-year-old range is edged by the Towaliga Fault to the northwest and Goat Rock Fault to the southeast. Dowdell's Knob in the distance.

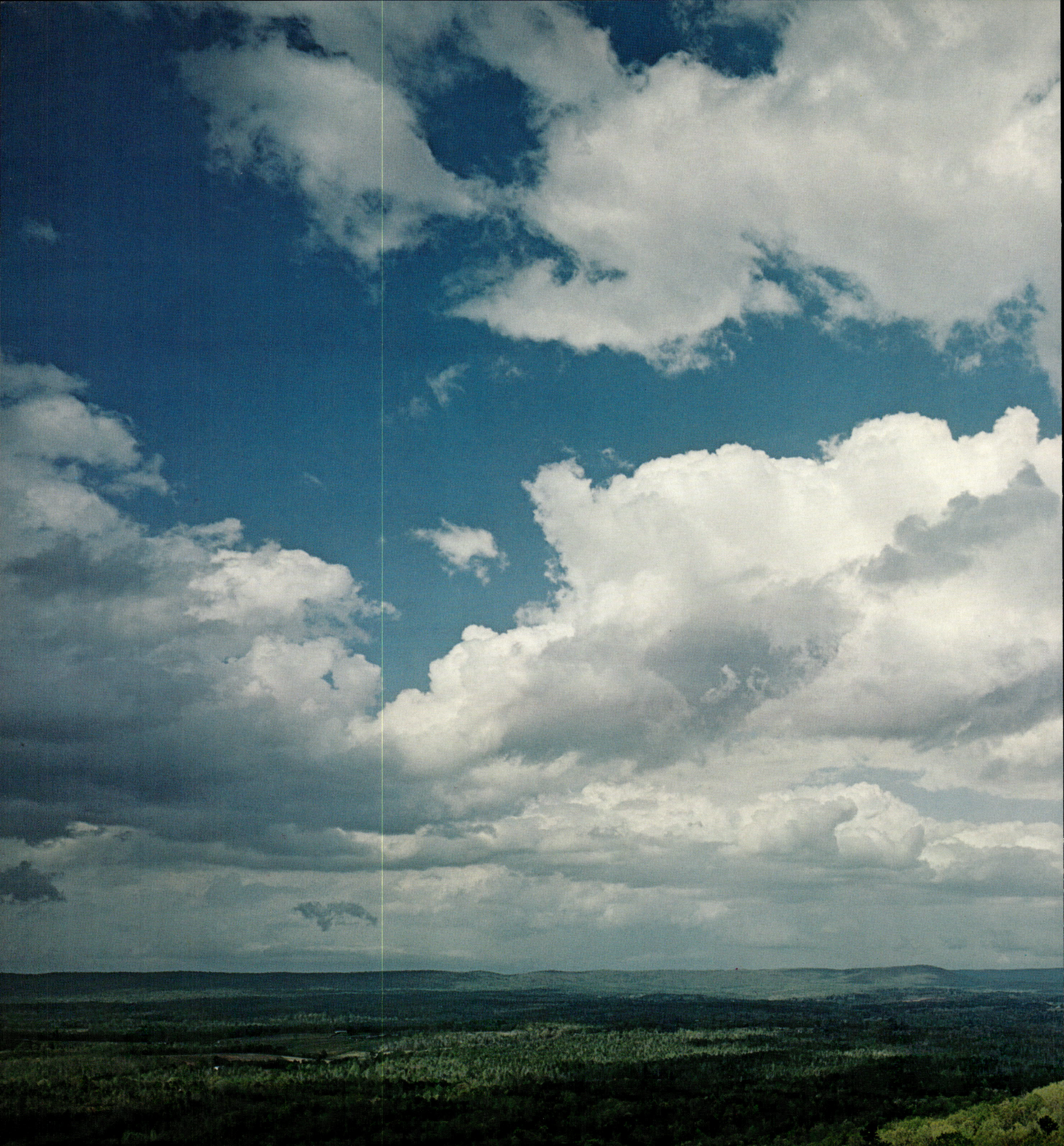

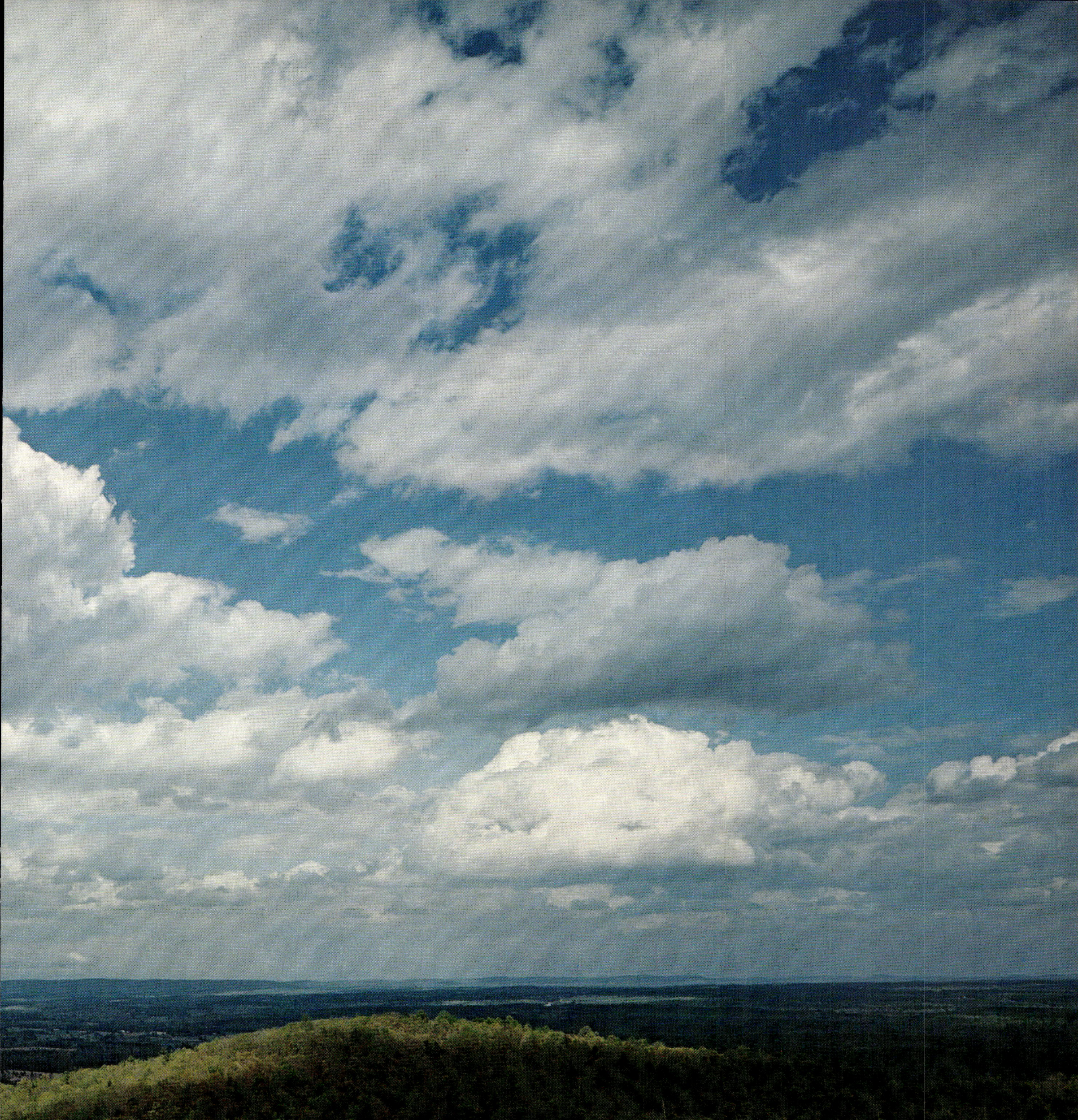

The broad Flint River vaporizes on a cool
summer morning near Thomaston. Right: In the
middle of Cornish Creek these tupelo gum trees
thrive on the nutritive clay-filled water
in the region of Covington.

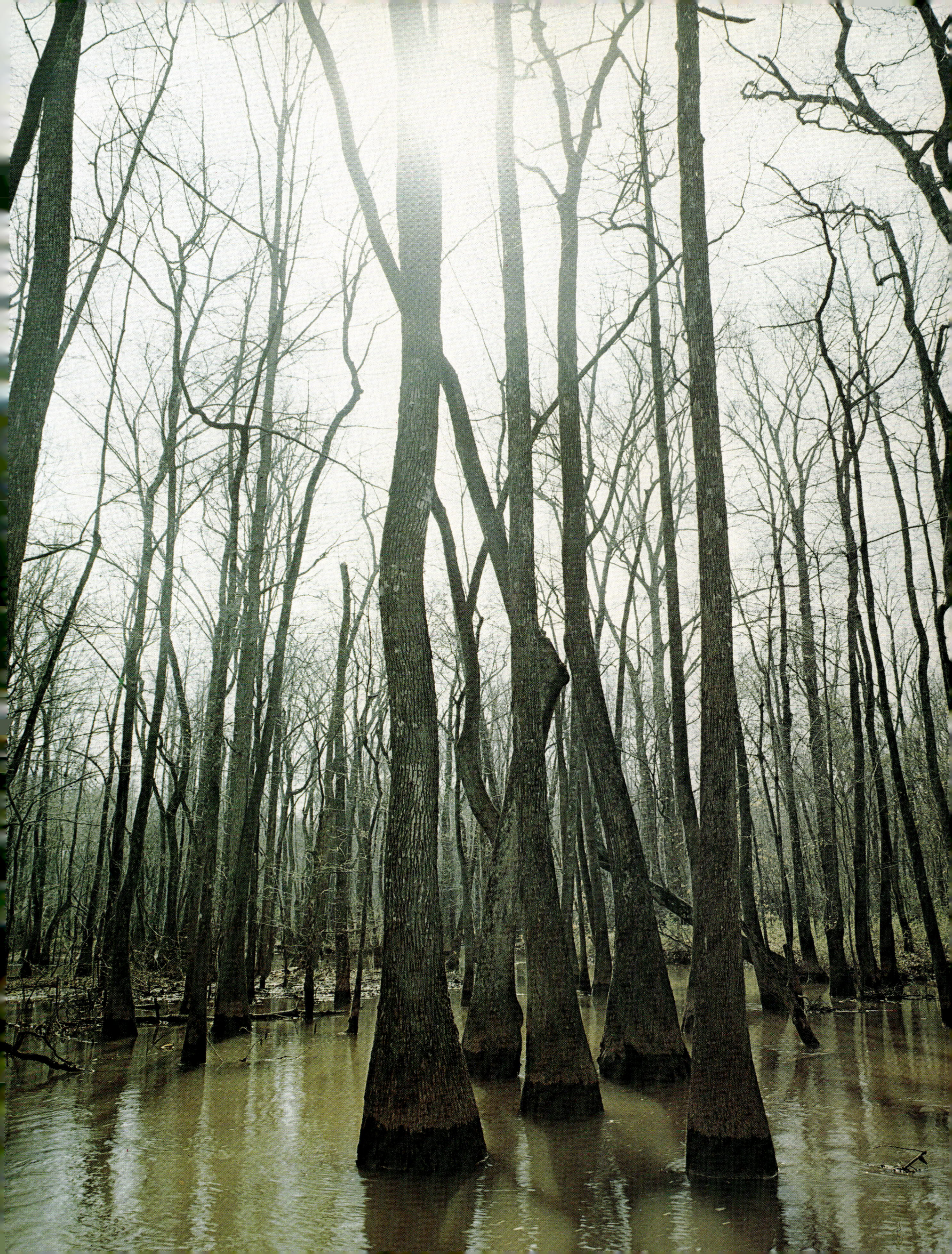

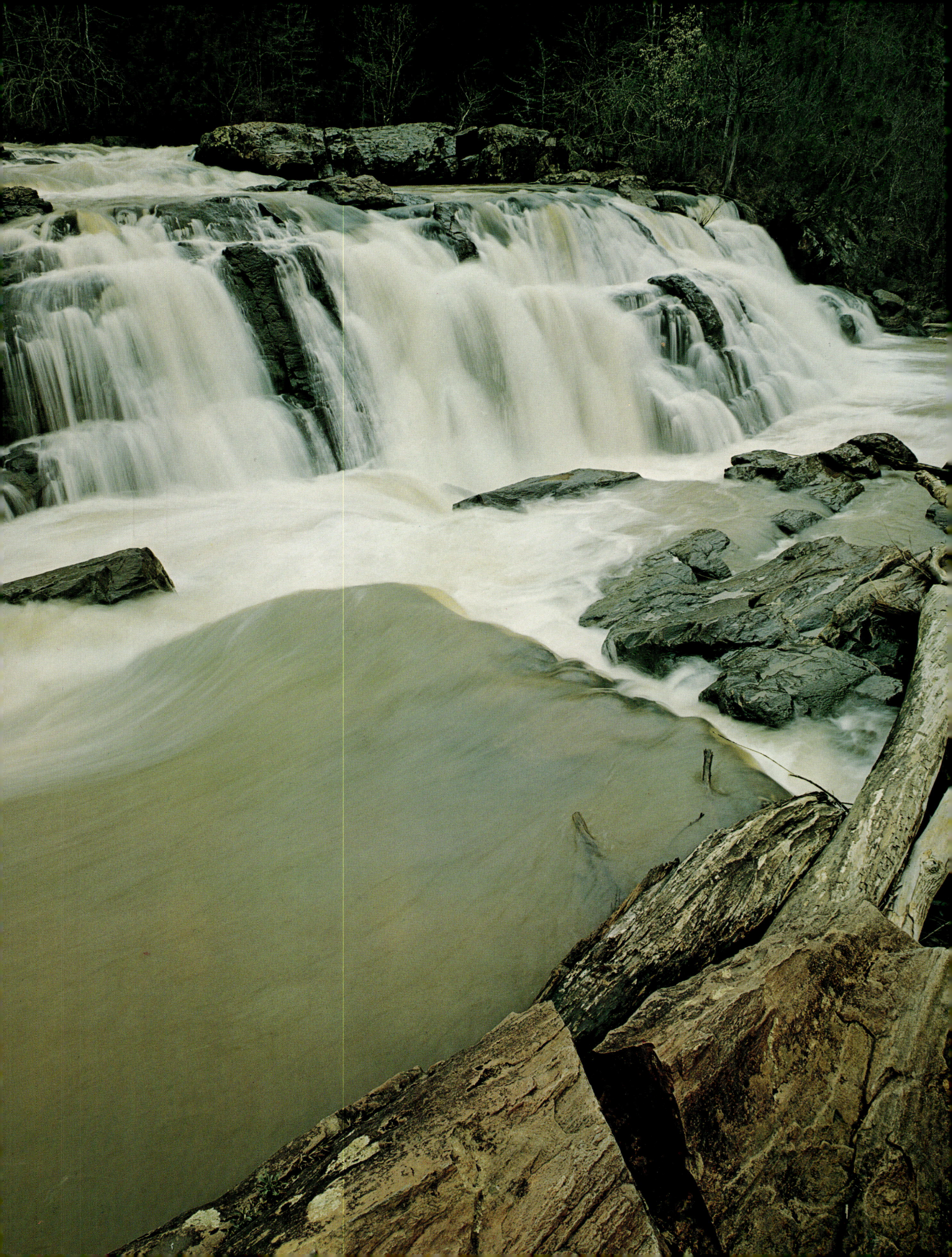

A remarkable display of redbud or Judas tree. This small leguminous understory tree confines itself principally to the Piedmont forests. Seen here in Cator Woolford Memorial Gardens, Cerebral Palsey Center, Atlanta.
Left: Out of Pine Mountain comes the unending waters of Mulberry Creek; Mulberry Grove.

Here on the famous thirteenth hole at Augusta another round of golf continues under a canopy of dogwood; site of the Augusta National Golf Tournament.

In early April a pageant of over 600 varieties of
azaleas begin to bloom at Callaway Gardens,
Pine Mountain.

The wild frothy Alcovy, cascades one more time
before joining Lake Jackson, near Covington.

Aquatic hooded pitcher plants with translucent windows nestle in small communities throughout the prairies of the Okefenokee National Wildlife Refuge. They have a slick lining that prevents insects from climbing back out, once in.

Deep in Beards Creek, a mysterious green glow
evokes spirits of the swamp near Glenville.

Below Spewrell Bluff, the rain swelled
Flint River flows past nearby Thomaston.
Pages 120 and 121: The torrential Towaliga
River roars along and appropriately accepts its
name, High Falls, High Falls State Park.

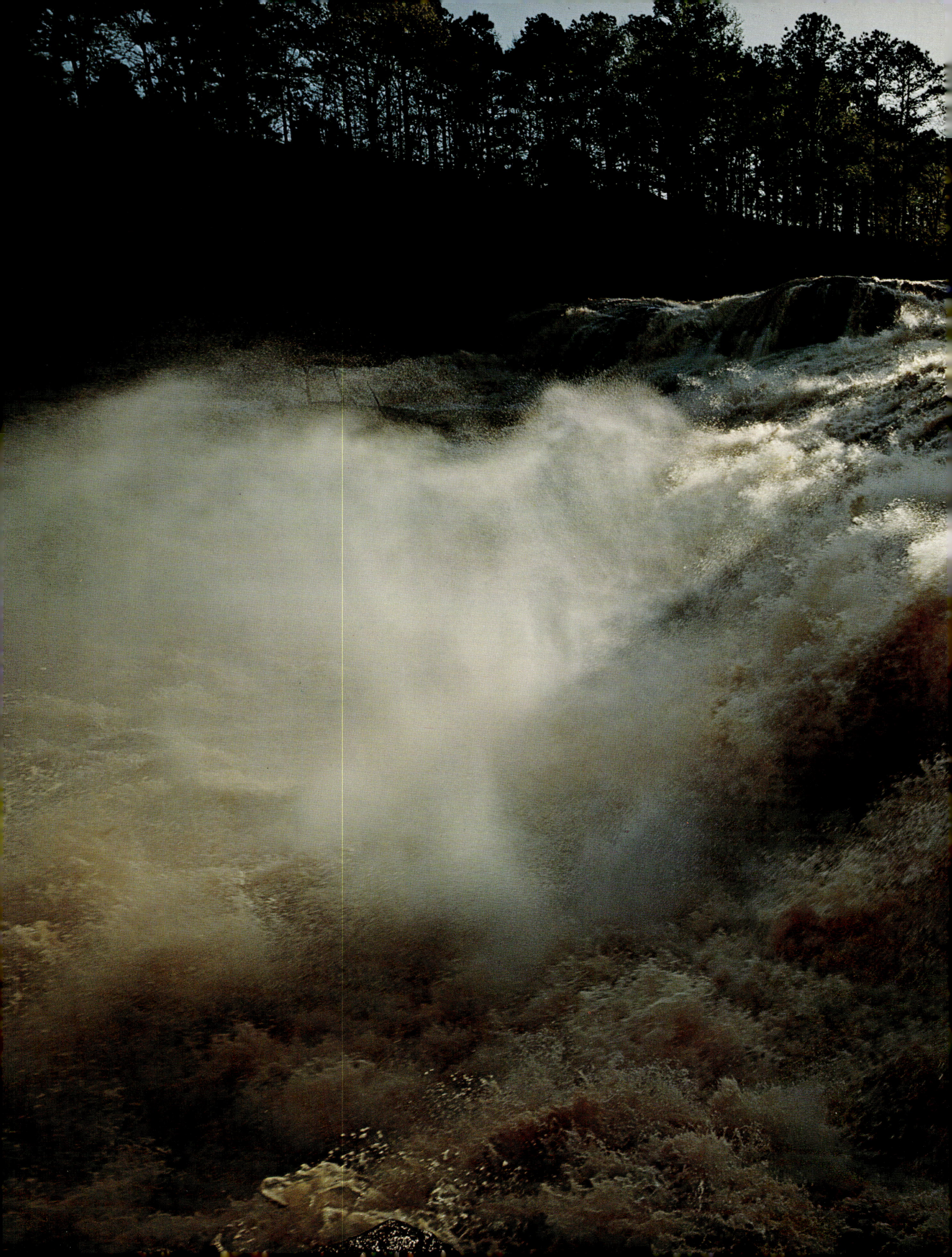

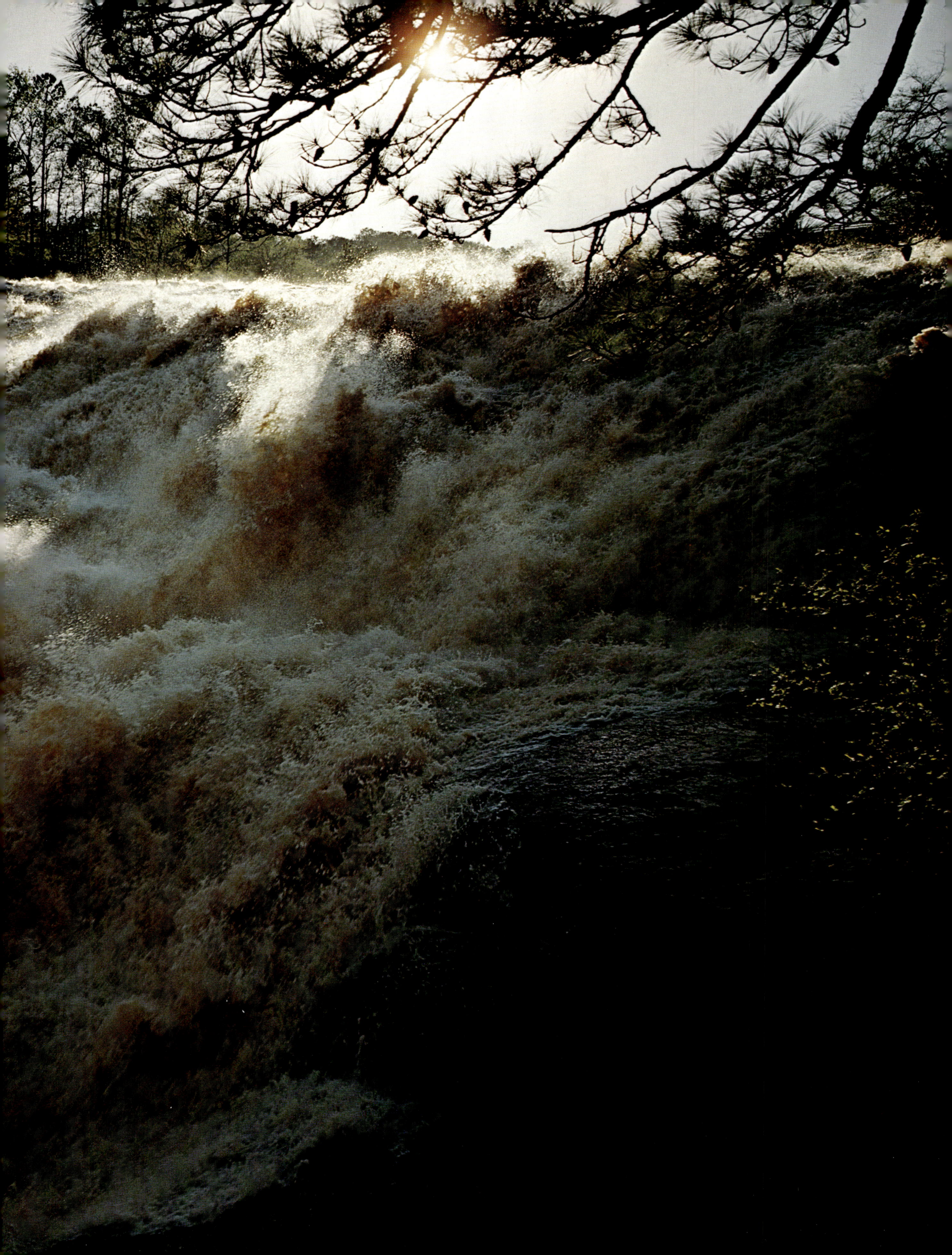

The natural foaming in the stream at Broxton Rocks is due to tannic acid in the water, which comes from the bark of trees and decaying plants. Acres of large porous fractured boulders surround this bubbling waterway near Broxton.

Time is lost, the water and sky are mirrored as one. You and your canoe become part of the sky; Okefenokee National Wildlife Refuge. Pages 124 and 125: For eons the ocean covered these bluffs. Now exposed fossil-laden banks of the Savannah River, are a geologic and botanic paradise, at Shell Bluff.

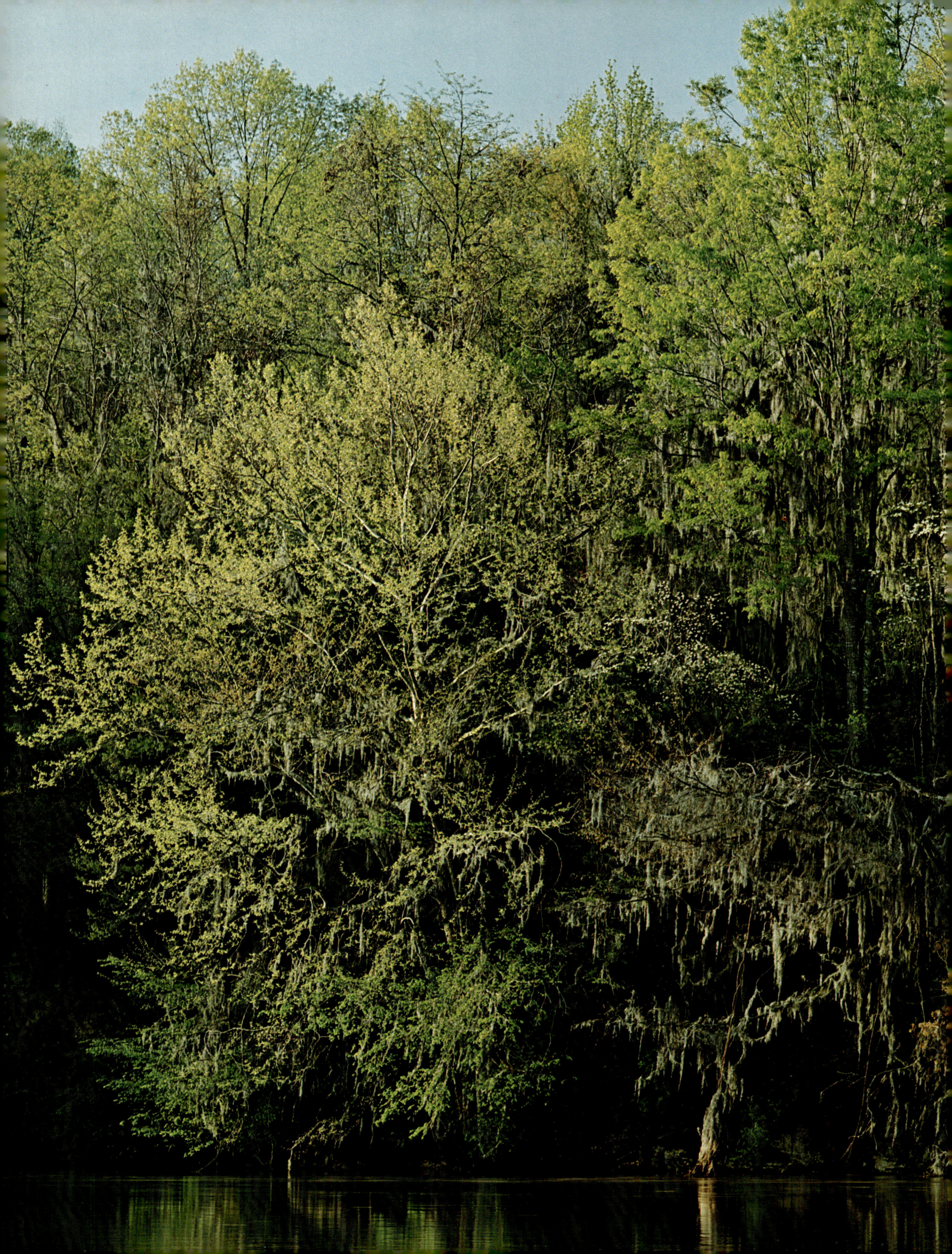

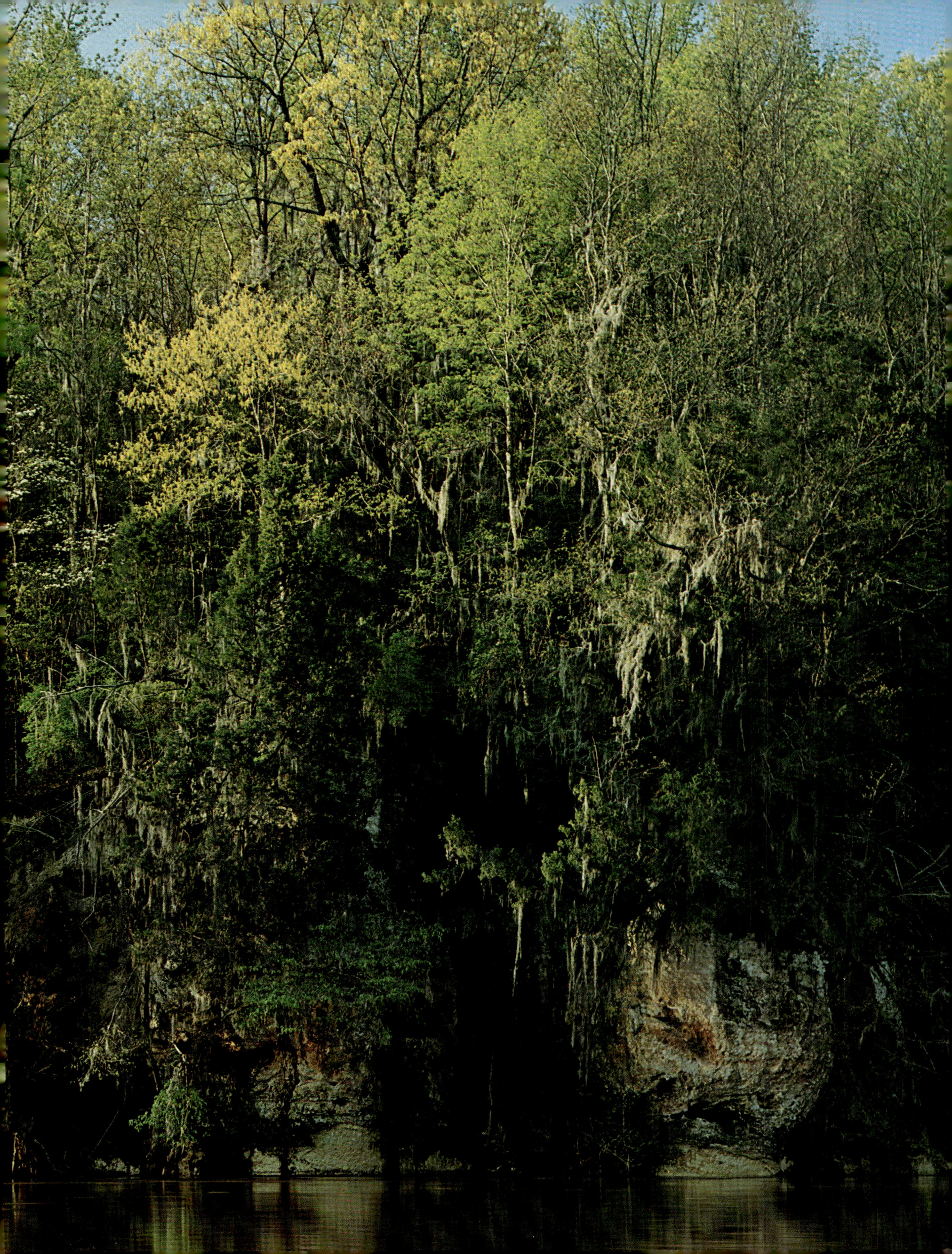

Yellow flowers provide a restful contrast within the Okefenokee National Wildlife Refuge.

A draped oak bows down to the
Savannah River with its costume of Spanish
moss below Shell Bluff.

This avenue of pond cypress peacefully awaits the fall mist to melt into rain. Middle Fork, Okefenokee National Wildlife Refuge near Stephen Foster State Park.

Glistening water dotted with lily pads,
low growing marsh grasses and cypress heads
dominate the great prairies of the
Okefenokee National Wildlife Refuge.

A most prehistoric-looking sandhill
crane spreads its wings to rest on a dead cypress.
Swamp moods above Big Water Lake,
Okefenokee National Wildlife Refuge.

The crystal waters of Spring Creek share
their world with an abundance of fish and a
Spanish moss-draped live oak, near Brinson.

At Goby Springs millions of gallons of crystal-clear water boil from this limestone grotto near Brinson. It retains a constant year-around temperature of 68 degrees Fahrenheit.

Ancient forest of pond cypress surrounds silent canoe as it moves with sun-filled energy from the blue canyons of space. Moods in the Okefenokee National Wildlife Refuge above Big Water Lake.

These carnivorous pitcher plants
appear in great abundance in the isolated
bogs of southwest Georgia, near Moultrie.

Brinson Springs, a spiritual watering hole for the giant bald cypress. Pages 136 and 137: Past fields of parched red clay and through thickets of slash pine glistens a true jewel. Brinson Springs, a crystalline spring grotto, is embraced in a setting of bald cypress and magnolia.

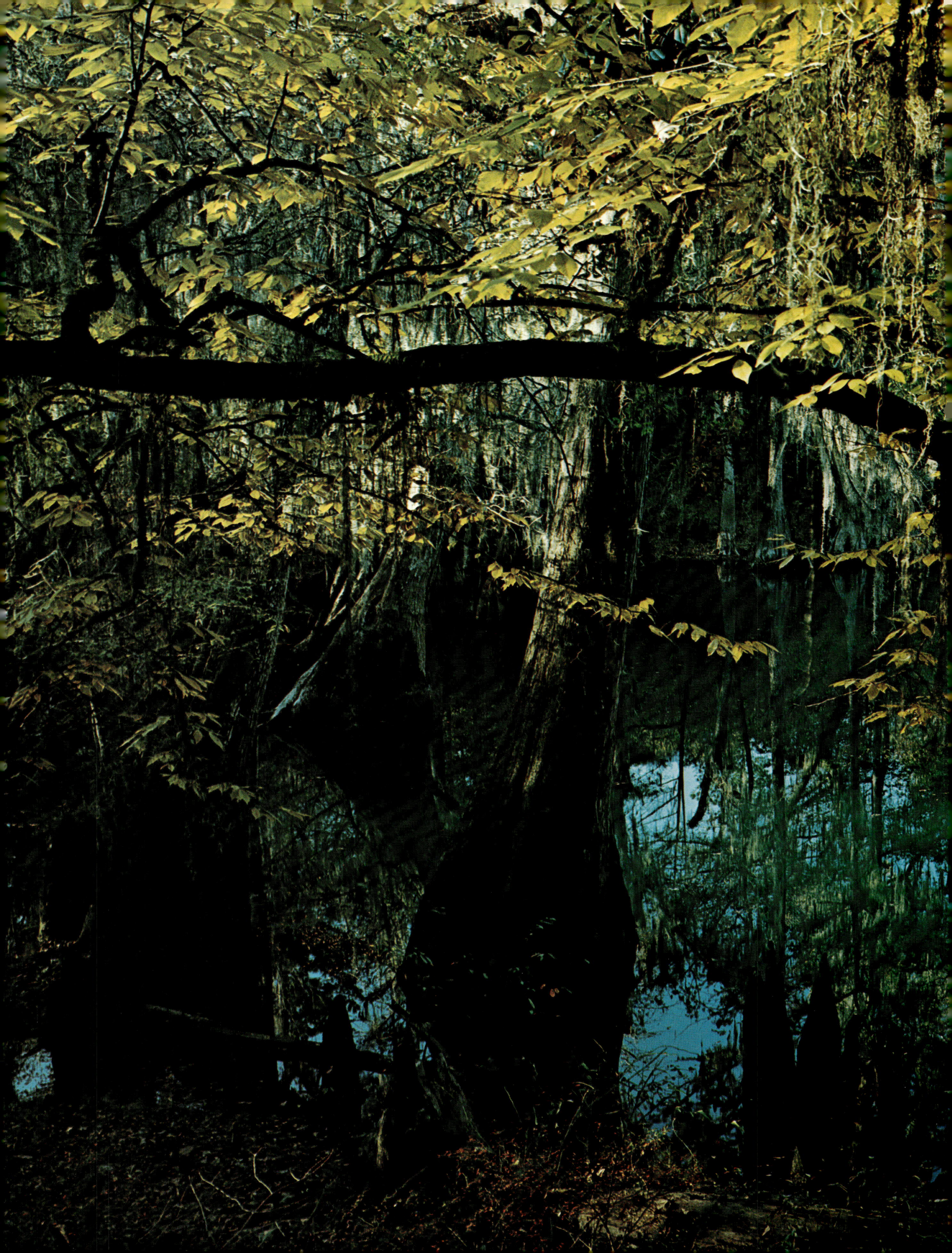

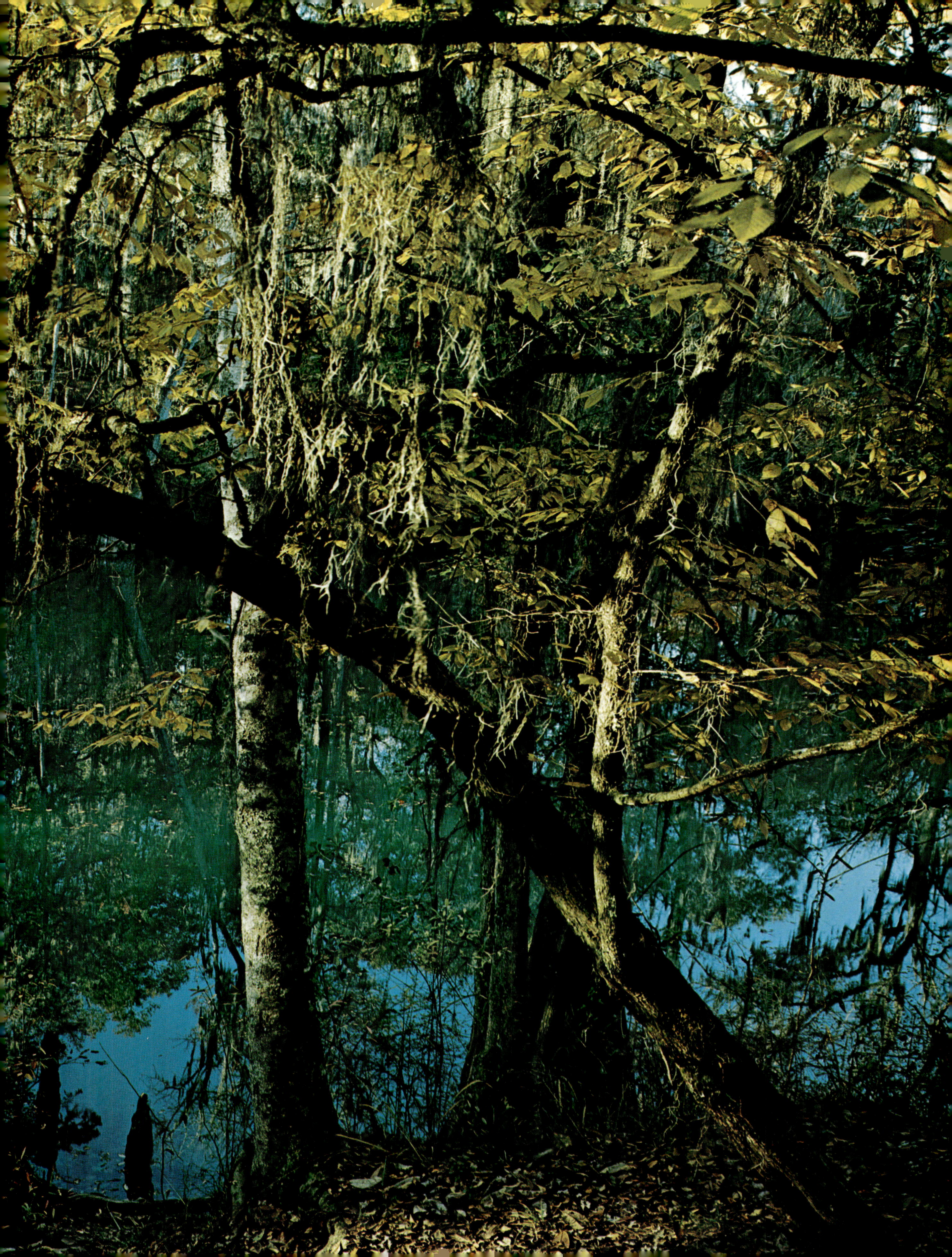

Knees from the submerged roots of cypress tree break the surface amidst a bubbling spring. This refreshing spring ultimately joins the Alapaha River between Mayday and Statenville.

Flat land in the area of Coheelee Creek, once a sea bottom, now tells us of an exposed undersea world slowly rising up and draining off its murky waters near Blakely. Pages 140 and 141: Silky smooth waters of Big Satilla River wind slowly on toward the Atlantic, State Highway Number 252, Folkston,

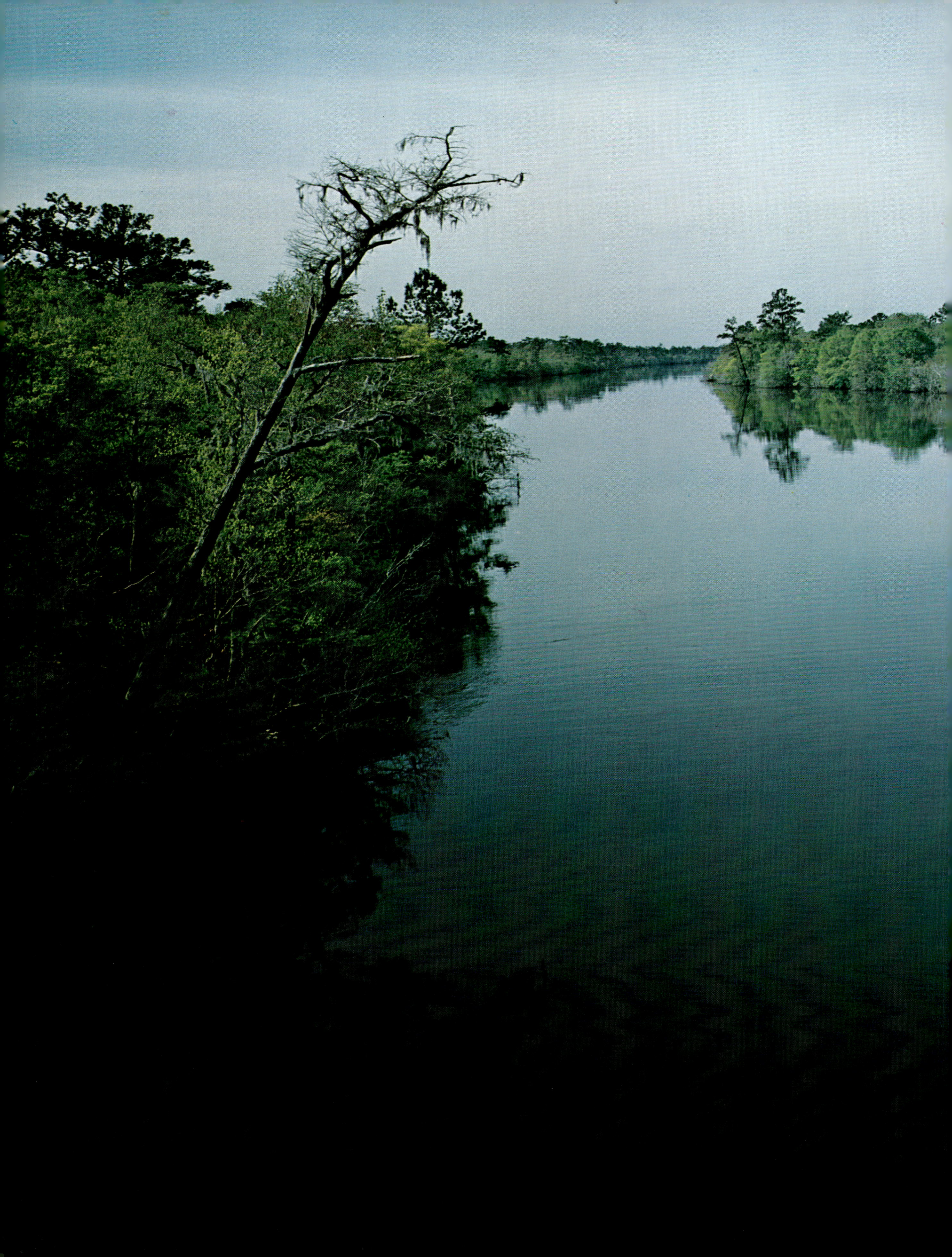

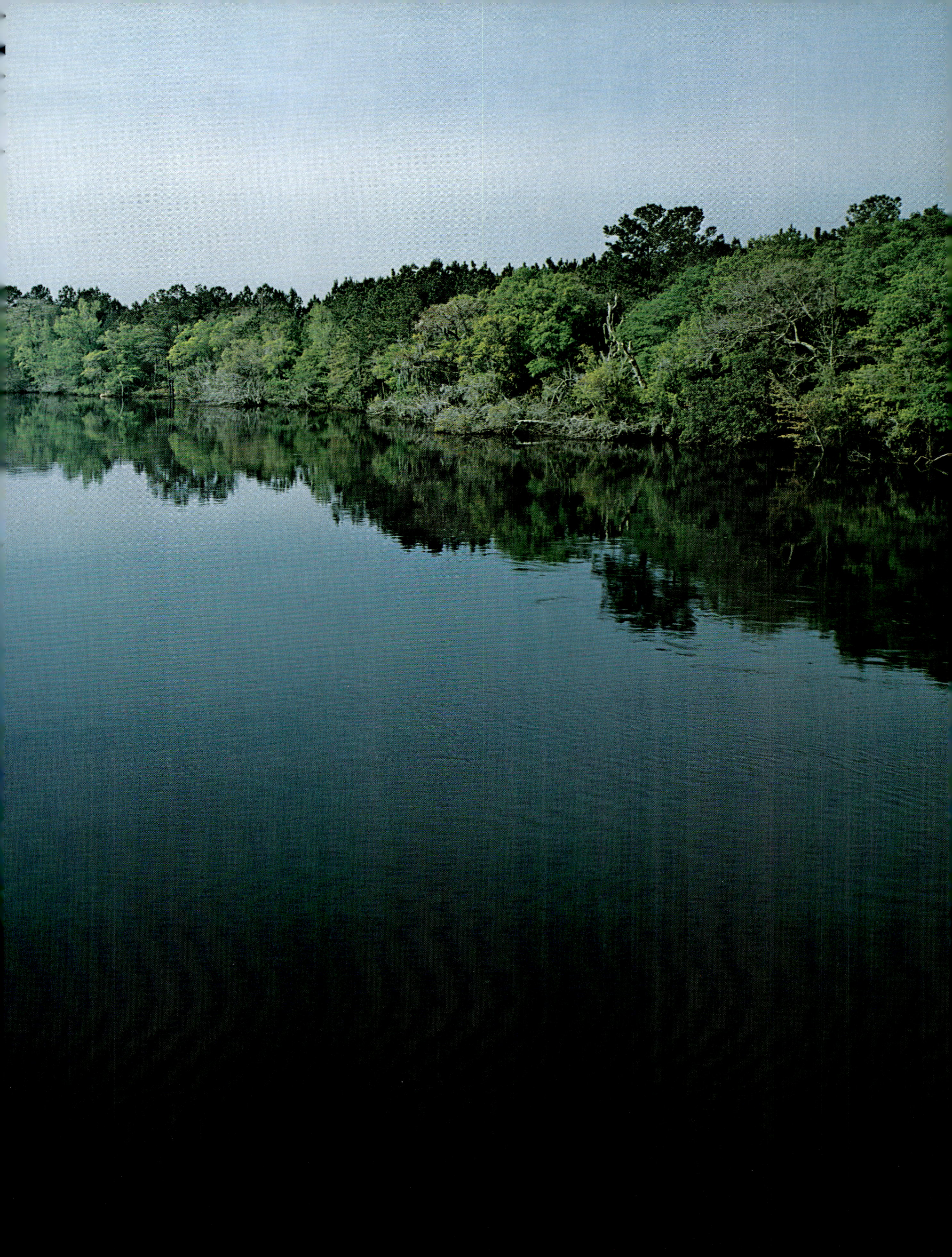

The great pyramid, Sacred Temple
Mound, of the Creek Indian nation still sands
in reverence to a culture whose life style
was in perpetual harmony with the earth.
Kolomoki State Park, near Blakely.

Within an hours drive from Plains, lies Providence Canyon. Through centuries of natural erosion the inner layering of the Coastal Plain is remarkably visible. This portion between canyon six and seven is called "Ships in the Harbor" because of the ribbed effect.

This lavish club on Jekyll Island once housed
the guests of millionaire J. P. Morgan, who came
to retreat on this island in the first part
of the century.

Well-preserved courthouse in Covington is a
prime example of Victorian architecture.
It was erected in 1884.

A young raccoon peers down from his tree house in Beard's Creek Swamp.

Near Folkston, along the banks of the
great Satilla River is a bluff permitting you to
touch massive magnolias that were
here before Columbus.

It is estimated that this noble bald cypress took
refuge on Lewis Island before the crusades.
The hiding place of these tree giants is on the
Altamaha River close to Darien.

The mirrored Altamaha River melts into the sky to be one with itself. Image near Rifle Cut Canal, Darien.

Rising from the lush carpet of herbs and bracken fern is the oldest long-leaf pine forest in the state (circa 250 years). Greenwood Plantation in Thomasville.

Deep in the brackish backwater of the Ebenezer Swamp area a cypress submerged in high water, is greater than 30 feet in diameter. The headless tupelo gum in the foreground appears to be leading a swamp symphony. Pages 152 and 153: St. Marys River, drifting toward an Atlantic estuary near Interstate Highway 95.

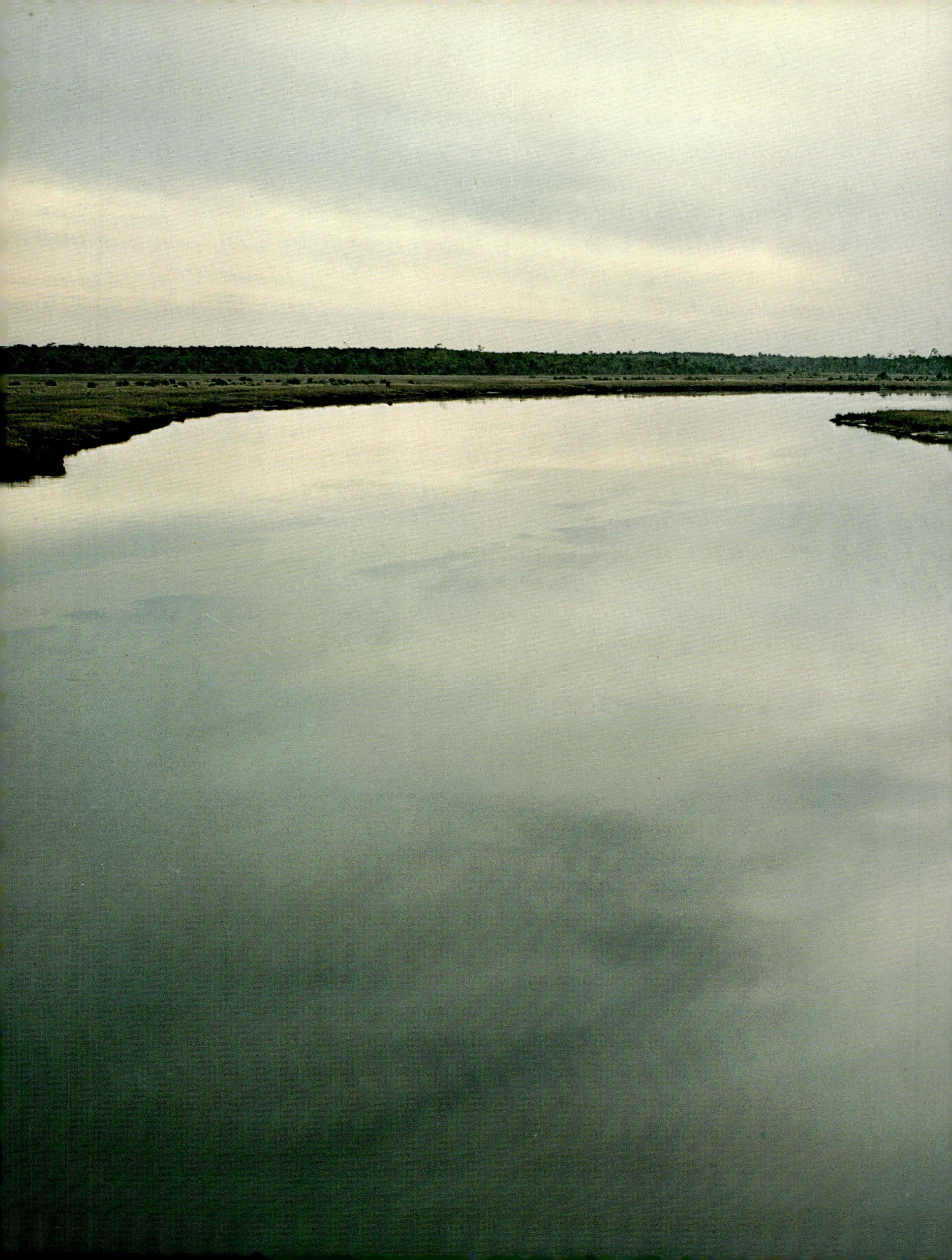

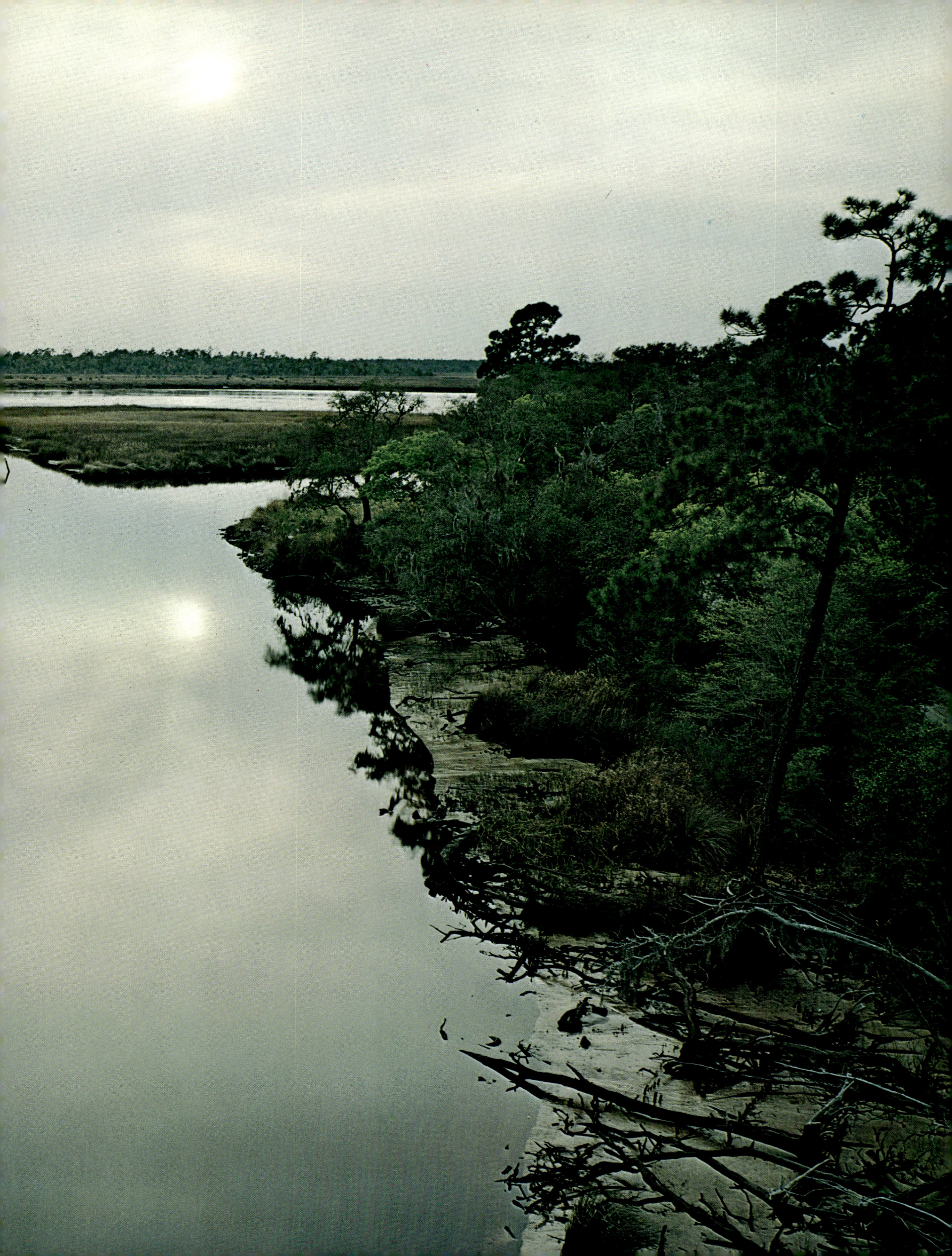

In the early moments of spring on the
Suwannee River your vision may be soaked with
a burst of the winged seeds of red maple,
outside Fargo.

154

The Okefenokee sends its tea-colored
water, filled with mellow vibrations of puffy
white clouds, to conceive the Suwannee River,
near the Florida border. Pages 156 and 157:
A bald cypress of undetermined age thrusts its
body across the banks of the Withlacoochee
River, near Valdosta.

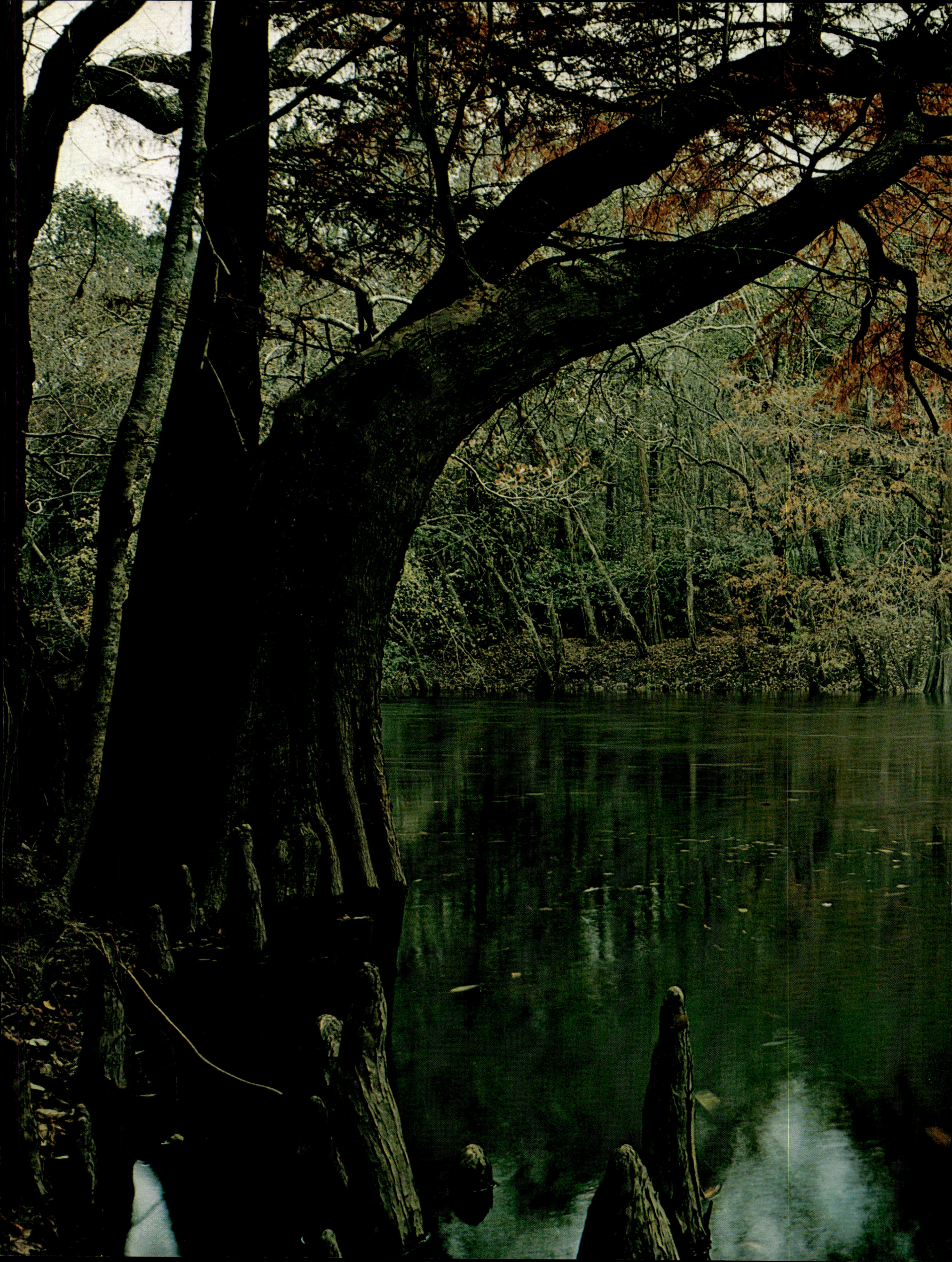

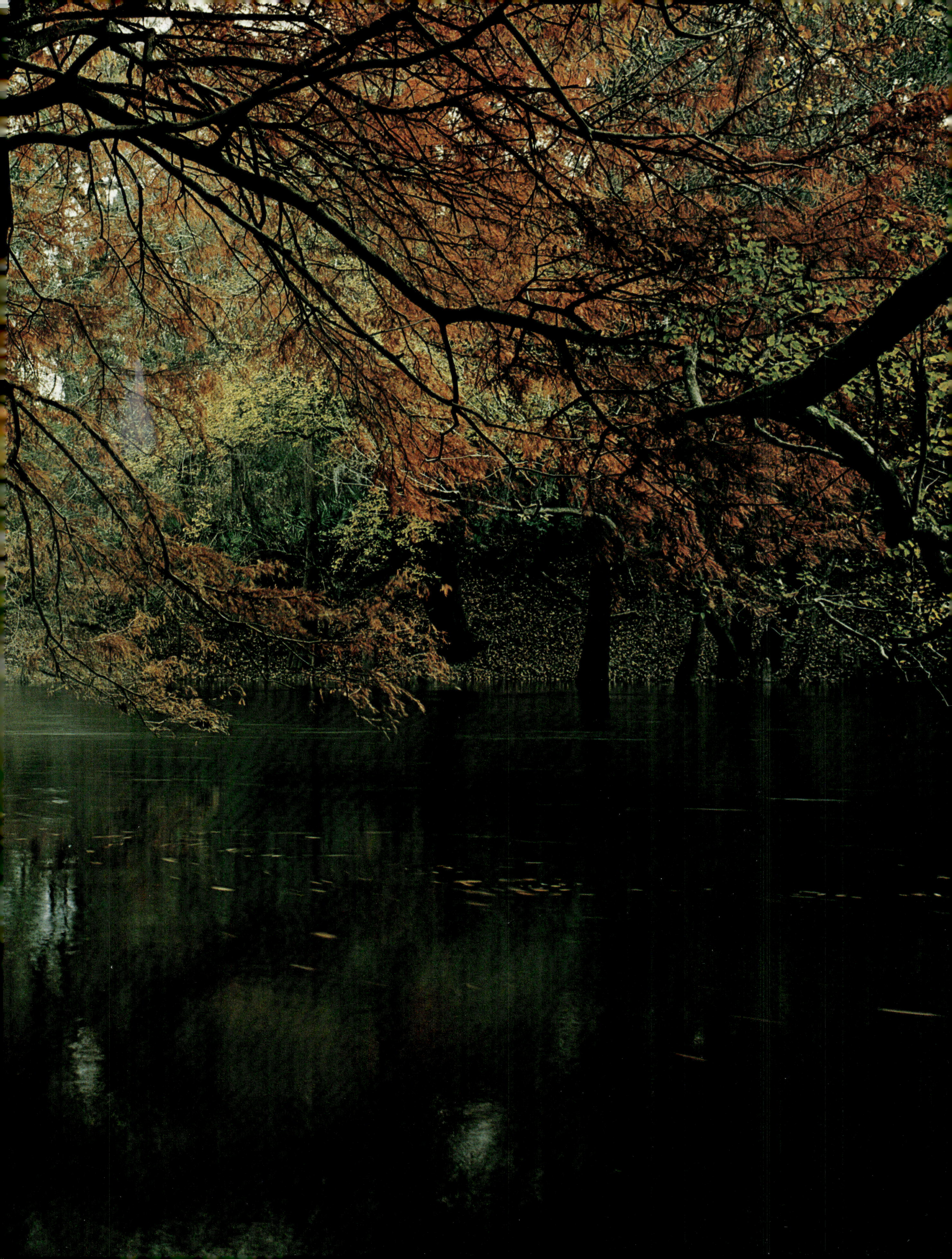

The early spring canoeist on the headwaters of the St. Marys River, forming part of the Georgia/Florida border, will occasionally experience a floral display of wild hoary azalea.

This gnarled ogeeche lime protrudes
above the waters of the Withlachoochee River.
Jellies are made from the large red fruits.
This tree replaces the tupelo gum on the
blackwater streams of the lower Coastal Plain,
in the area of Valdosta.

East of the Ohoopee River is a dwarf oak-evergreen shrub forest. The oaks, with yellow leaves, are often called turkey oak, because they resemble a turkey's track. The unique shrub (left foreground) is rosemary. The pale green plants are two species of woody mints with red and purple flowers. State Highway 152, Cobbtown.

This blue-gray sculpture is the very top portion
of a weathered live oak tree that was protruding
from the pinnacle of a 60 foot sand dune,
Cumberland Island National Seashore.

Expanding sand dunes are slowly encroaching on this duckweed-filled swamp in Cumberland Island National Seashore.

In late March the lush semi-tropical gardens
of the Glynn County Courthouse, Brunswick,
explode with azalea blossoms. Built in 1907,
it depicts the delightful architecture of that era.

Swamp palmetto highlighted with a splash
of late evening light, on Ossabaw Island.

This noble live oak, reflects the spirit of an ancient sentinel, remembering when it was an integral part of the great plush forests that once dominated this area. Image within Cumberland Island National Seashore.

Dipping its head out of the blue heavens
this wood horse spirit savors a bit of the
Jekyll Island marsh grass.

Live oak projects thousand-pound arms seeking perfect balance and light on Jekyll Island. Pages 168 and 169: Zones of marsh vegetation reveal variations of plants, primarily due to increase in elevation. In the distance is yellow spartina marsh grass, center, dark marsh plants and wax myrtle, on St. Catherine's Island.

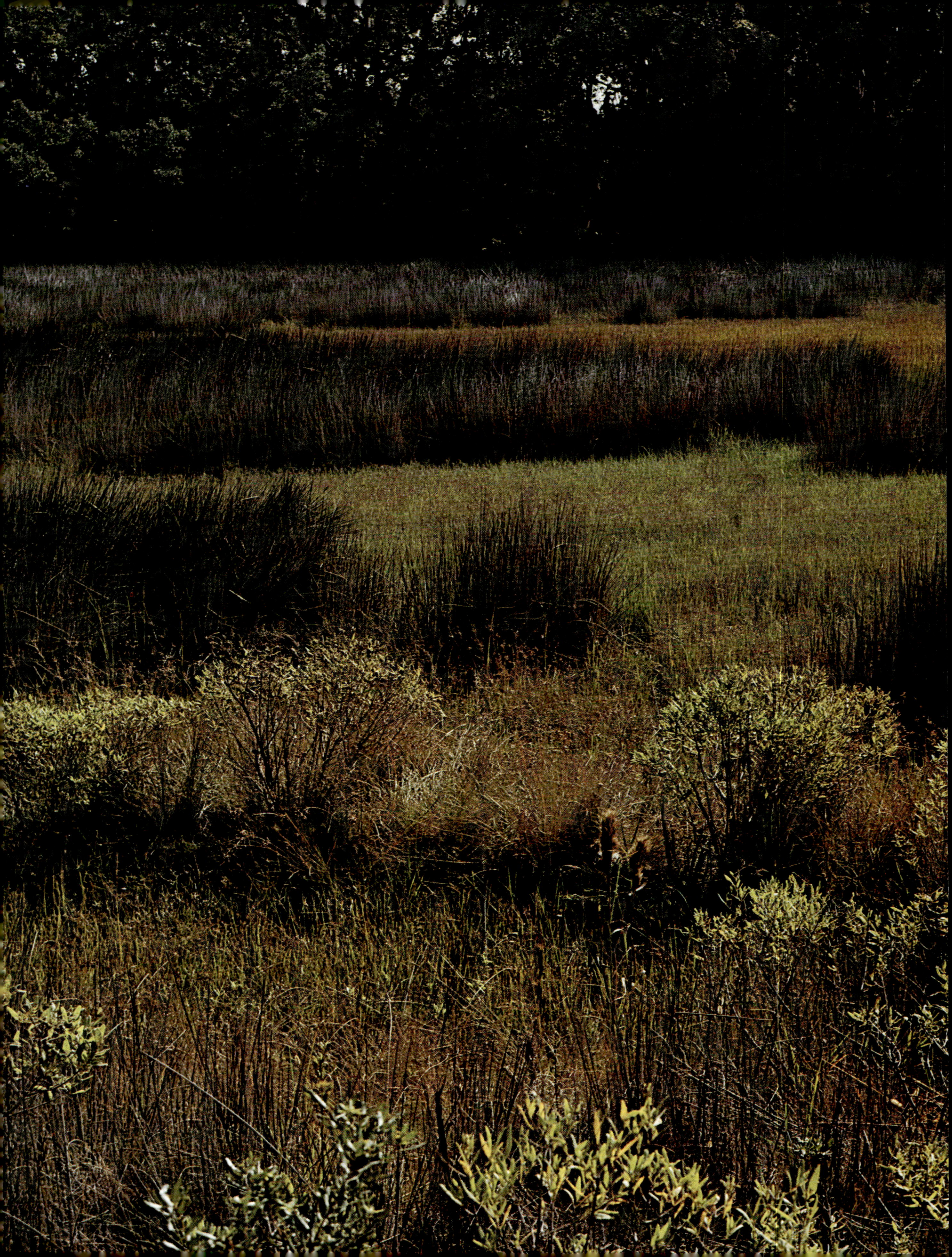

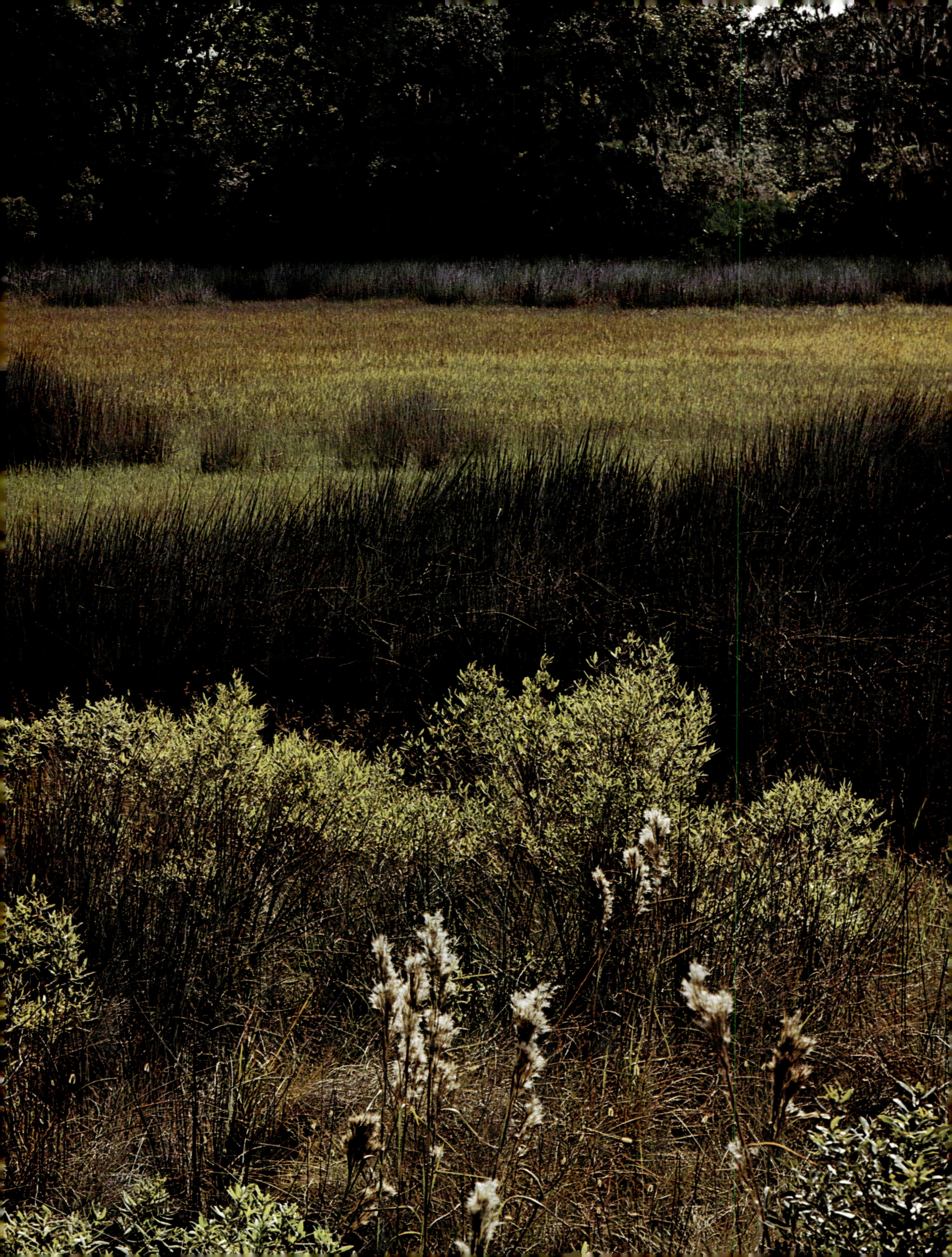

This distinctive live oak presides near the shore of Lake Whitney, the largest natural freshwater lake on the coastal islands; Cumberland Island National Seashore.

Three mid-successional sand dune plants, coastal island cedar, prickly pear and wax myrtle anchor the sands on Sapelo Island. Pages 172 and 173: Fog essence rhythmically blends the oaks and sea together as one expression of life. Viewed from highest dune on the coastal shore, Cumberland Island National Seashore.

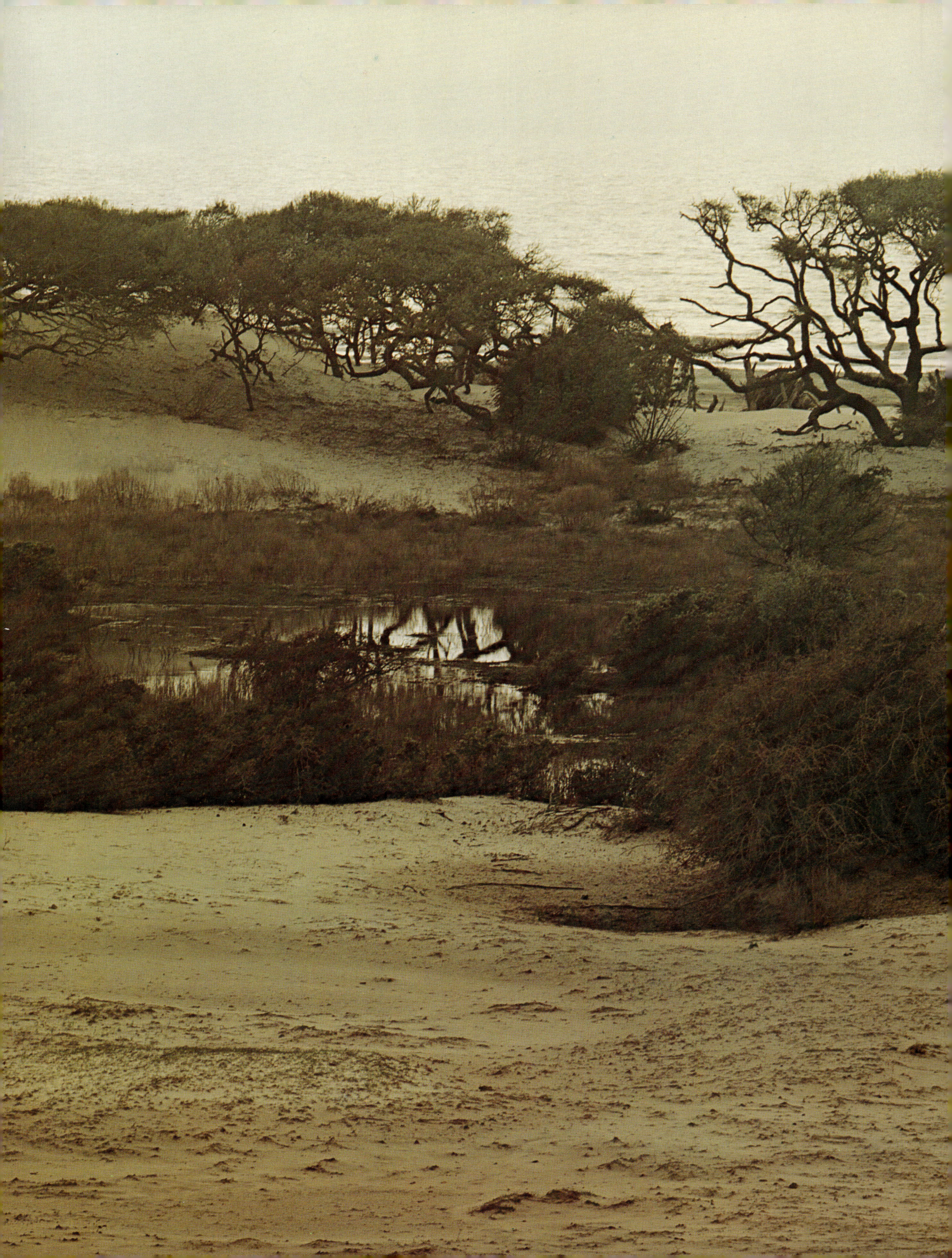

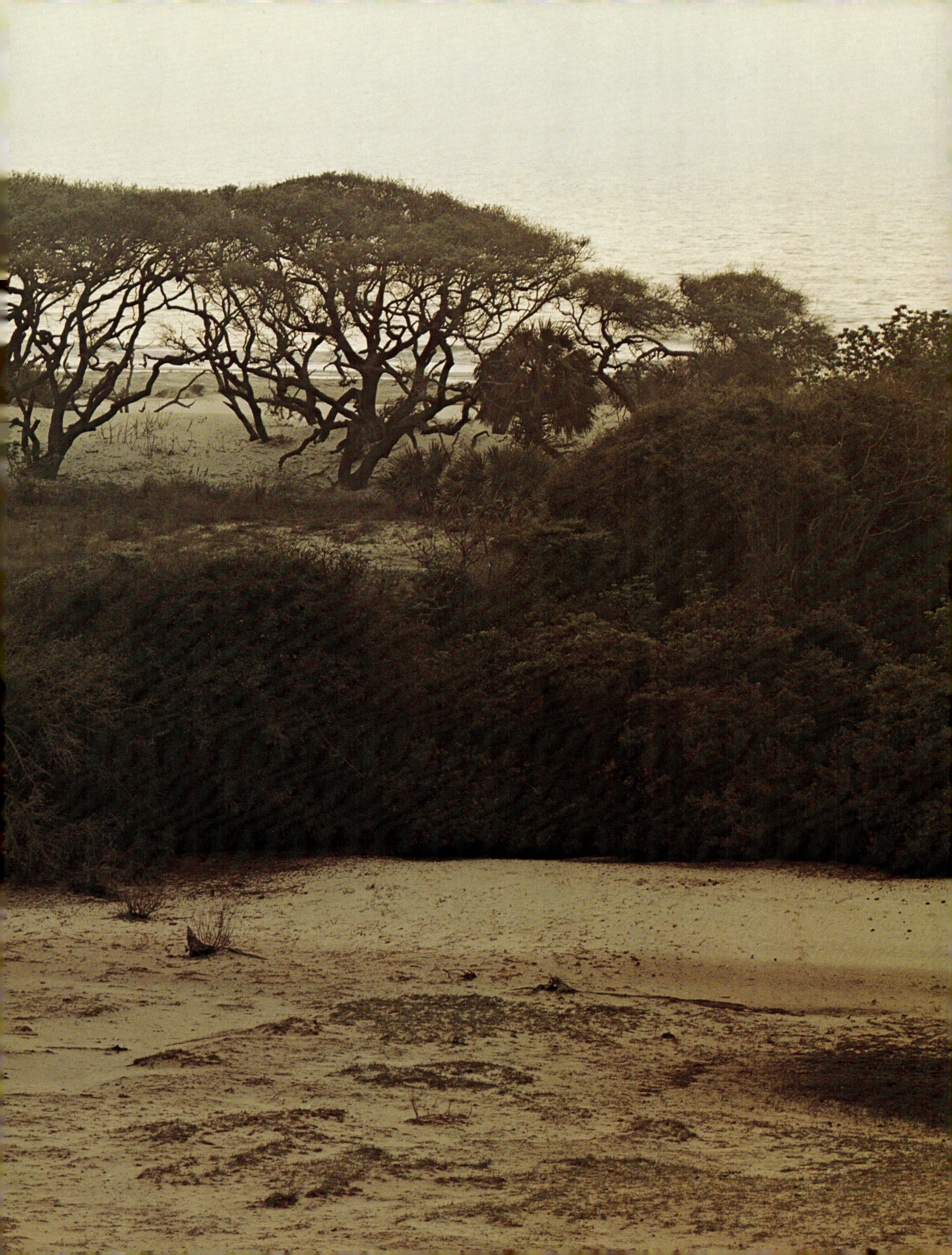

Cabbage Garden Creek is among thousands
of tidal saltwater systems which gather nutrients
from the marshes to feed the sea, along the
shore of Ossabaw Island.

Surrounded by the security of cattails,
these mallards prepare their summer home in
the Savannah Wildlife Refuge.

Dripping spartina grass slowly lifts its stalks
out of an ascending fog on Cat Head Creek,
near Darien.

Mid-day sun highlights a labyrinthian maze of marsh grass and tidal creek fingers; Tybee Marsh aerial, Savannah.

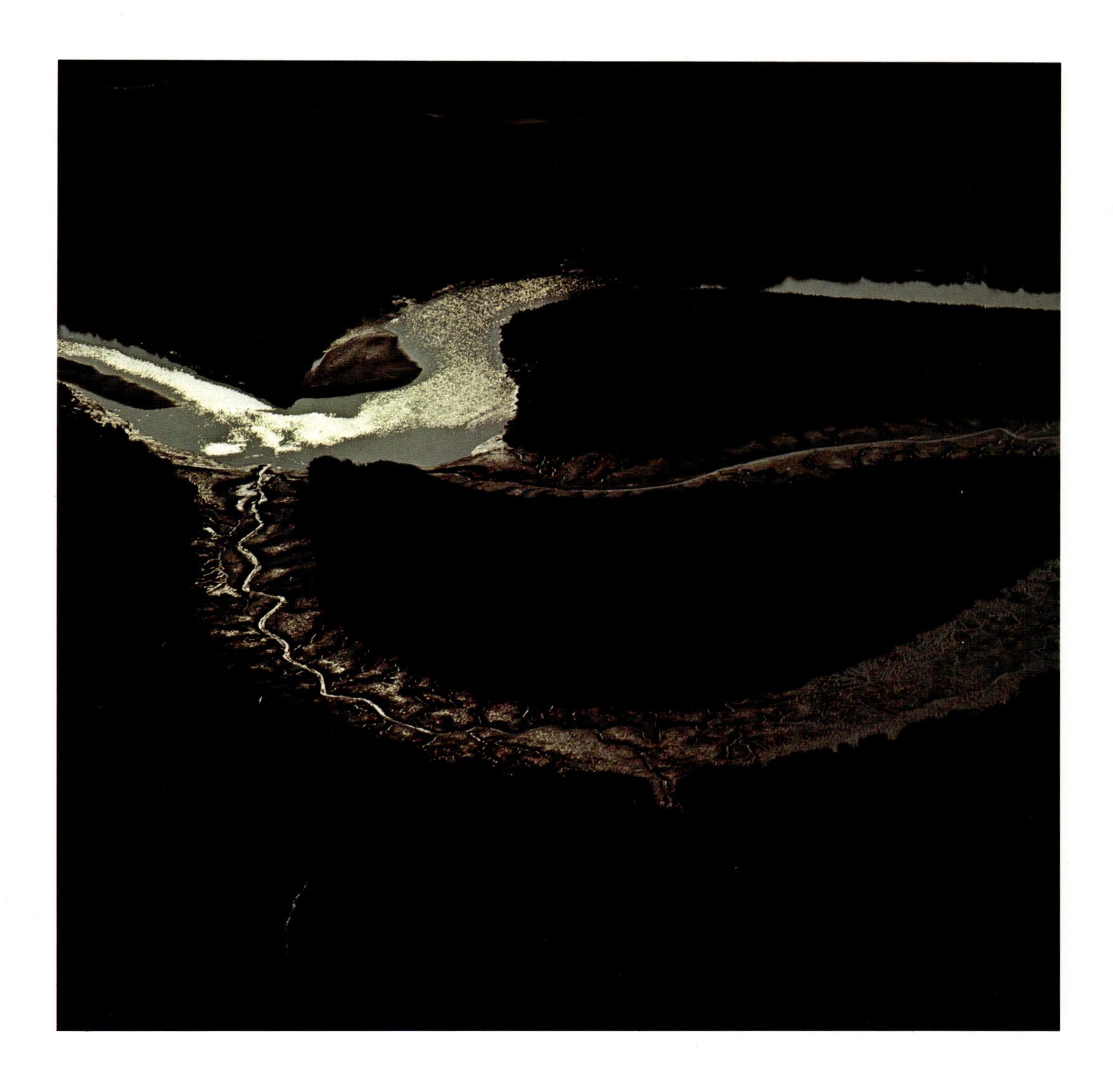

The ebb of time splashes on the tiny
aligned feet of these senectuous mariners;
Cumberland Island National Seashore.

178

Amidst succulent glassworts on Oldner Island there is a soft egret feather, reminder of how all things must eventually flow back into mother earth.

Man returns to the sea on the blue waves
of hope and good fortune; Wassaw Island.

Driven by the swirling forces of the wind
from the sea, the sand slowly covers the marshes
of the south end of Big Cumberland Island.

The power of the sea is wrenched out
of the sand, the power of the rained-soaked oak
is whirled back into the sea. Image on
South End Beach, Ossabaw Island.

With undiminished wisdom this live oak
bows with the evening glow; Cumberland
Island National Seashore. Pages 184 and 185:
Delicate world of form, spartina grass
on Ossabaw Island.

This intricate wetland swamp-marsh is one
of the richest food-producing systems on earth.
Truly an aerial microcosmic study of
the world; Ossabaw Island.

Waiting long enough and quietly
enough, miracles happen on the edge of the sea;
Cumberland Island National Seashore. Pages
188 and 189: Infinite marshes girding west side
of Ossabaw Island provide perfect buffer
zone protecting mainland from hurricanes
and establishes a nursery for the sea.

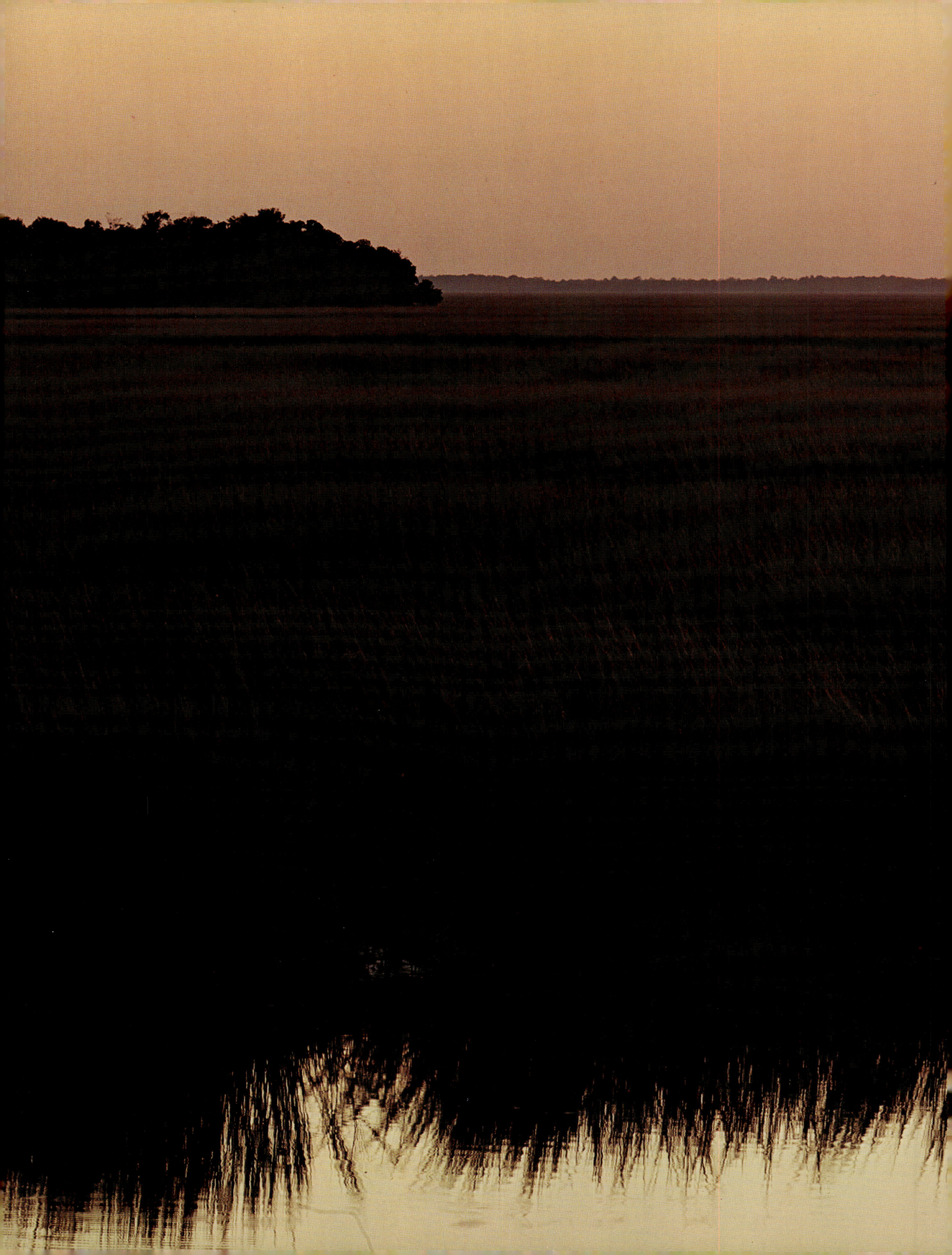

The golden ember sun voyages across the dunes
on the north end of Big Cumberland Island.

Twisted oak reaches up to witness a winter storm only to stand motionless as the swirling sand and rain carve its future. Image within Cumberland Island National Seashore, that covers 36,876 acres.

GEORGIA
Landscapes of the Mind

In completing this book a unique part of my life has witnessed the undiminished and nourishing flow of our wilderness. My vision path into a soft land overflowing with a microcosmic cross section of the universe has filled me with an intrinsic wealth of earth knowledge. The skin of Georgia has evolved through a billion years of growth and change. Each change has been of divine order, molding a diversity of life that is unequaled anywhere else in the world. Unlike the (yang) thrusting landscape energy of the rugged Tibetan Himalayas, which is on our same latitude, this state exudes a very (yin) yielding and soft landscape energy. In the early sixties was my first encounter with that soft landscape, a state whose mountains have become very rounded and mellow, whose Piedmont has become a gradual slope once opening onto an ancient sea and whose coast remains in a celebrant mood, sharing with the world the wildest shore line in Eastern America. In late 1969 I began my photographic quest to discover the unknown along our golden coast. A three-year odyssey initiated me into the ebb and flow of life on 17 major islands, plus 100 minor islands and nine major rivers. My next attempt to seriously absorb the landscape began in 1975. For over two and one-half years, I explored various ways that the (yin) energy flowed from the mountains to the sea. I chose water as that medium of travel. This book hopefully portrays that story, a water path from the heart of the soft Appalachian Mountains through the Piedmont and down into the Coastal Plain, only to eventually meet the sea.

Water Path to the Sea

Through a small opening in foggy space, a single drop of water gently settles on a swaying fern deep in the Cohutta Wilderness, a start, a beginning (cover). We are surrounded by water in the mountains. Its mystical clouds hover over yawning buttercups; its flow curls out of limestone caverns that honeycomb the inner workings of Lookout Mountain; its tiny bubbles effervesce at the base of giant boulders on the wild Chattooga as if to say, I hold the power, I am the only water, I am life.

Let us be water, find your way now, curl yourself into plump radiant rainbows, cascade with your melty friends down golden rocky canyons, seek mellow reflection pools so you can mirror the sky, freeze yourself into crystals on the pinnacles of mountains and release yourself as fog ascending from damp forested valleys. Join your traditional canopy home—the heavens.

All of these experiences are part of your body, you are absorbed into every fiber of the land and the creatures that inhabit the earth. You realize no barriers, even though your spirit is occasionally broken while waiting to pass over a textureless dam. You continue your journey out of the mountains and into the mighty rivers of the Piedmont. You pass through the throbbing towns and cities of man, helping purify the American way, "profit in the waste." As in centuries past, your power rests in the words of John M. Kauffman *(Flow East),* "rivers have what man most respects and longs for in his own life and thought—a capacity for renewal and replenishment, continual energy, creativity, cleansing." Your water energy now moves quickly over and around the egg-shaped monolith, Stone Mountain, your body is vaporized on hot summer mornings over the Flint River, you become almost motionless on your trek through the slow moving rivers of the Piedmont. Slowly your syrupy wetness starts to be absorbed into the most complex filtering system in the world, the great primordial swamp, the Okefenokee. The Coastal Plain, with its ancient swamps and crystalline springs, divides your consciousness. Some of your wetness becomes tea-colored rivers, other water spirits mix with ochre-colored clay from the north, and other waters come gushing out of surface springs to join the search for the sea. The water dance is almost complete. Your fluidness swells, becomes great river basins and deltas. Your destiny is now to empty your largess into the marshes and semi-tropical islands. Here in the marshes your waters provide a home for the sea nursery. Conducted by trillions of water particles, your water symphony carries the newborn life to melt into a single drop in space, the sea. You have finished the cycle.

I dedicate this book to Christine, an eternally lovely lady whose spirit celebrated its birth, and to all people, plants, and animals seeking life in peace with their mates, their environment.

With great respect, gratitude and special thanks, I wish to acknowledge the following organizations that helped make this book become possible:

The Georgia Conservancy
The Garden Club of Georgia
Georgia Department of Natural Resources
Georgia Forestry Commission
Georgia Power Company
National Parks Service
United States Forest Service

My love goes out to all the people who have been so generous with their time and energy, and assisted in the birth of "Georgia."

This book is a grain of sand reflecting with the most precious gift to us all—a pristine borderless Georgia, free to celebrate life in harmony with the divine flow of the universe.

James P. Valentine